BARING IT ALL

MEN IN CHARGE
BOOK 4

TORY BAKER

Cover Design by Kat Lopez

Editor Julia Good with Diamond in the Rough Editing

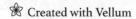 Created with Vellum

*Find someone who grows flowers in the darker
parts of you.
Zach Bryan*

PLAYLIST

Baring It All Playlist

Wild as Her by Corey Kent
Rush Rush by Paula Abdul
Jersey Giant by Evan Honer, Julia DiGrazia
I'm Not Pretty by Megan Moroney
Dawns by Zach Bryan, Maggie Rogers
Your Heart Or Mine by Jon Pardi
She's Alright by Zach Bryan
In Your Love by Tyler Childers
Sleeping Alone by Flatland Cavalry
Please Don't Go by Wyatt Flores
Chain Smokin' by Morgan Wallen
Losing Sleep by Wyatt Flores
Settle Me Down by Josh Abbot Band

A Life Where We Work Out by Flatland
Cavalry, Kaitlin Butts
Wasn't That Drunk by Josh Abbot Band, Carly
Pearce
Boots on a Dance Floor by Jon Wolfe

WARNING

This book contains a cheating ex-fiancee but don't worry Daddy Griff will take care of Stormy.

BLURB

I live life for the thrills and Stormy is straight
adrenaline.
She goes straight to my... heart.

If there's one girl out there I shouldn't mess
with, it's Stormy.
Everything about her screams off limits.
She's too young, hurting from being screwed
over, and my niece's best friend.

Don't get me wrong, I'm no saint.
But this girl is the biggest temptation I've
ever had.
That's anything but good—especially in the
small town we live in.

When her world is turned upside down on what was supposed to be her wedding day, I come to her rescue. As we walk out of the venue together, her dress in shambles, a bottle of tequila in one of her hands, and holding onto me with the other, tongues start wagging.

Stormy doesn't seem to care. I can't say I do either.

The longer I'm near her, the deeper I get. For once in my life, I'm not looking for a thrill, or even freedom.
I just want her.

PROLOGUE

ONE WEEK EARLIER

Stormy

"Harder, yes, right there." I stop in my tracks. I know that voice. Sounds like my best friend is hooking up with one of the groomsmen. Which sucks because I need her. This godawful dress I somehow was roped into wearing at this godawful ceremony, not to mention the godawful amount of people. Attention, good or bad, is not my idea of fun. Three hundred people, mostly Zach's family, conglomerates, and half the fucking town. Yeah, no freaking thanks. Except I got railroaded by Zach's mom. A force to be reckoned with, wearing me so far down it was easier to agree than stand my ground.

"Fuck yeah, you like being my dirty little secret, don't you, Mel." Ice runs through my veins. I fucking know that voice, too. That voice behind the heavy wooden door, inside this monstrosity of a ceremony location, a freaking clubhouse. I wanted a small intimate wedding with friends and family, one hundred people max. My hand goes to my chest, making sure my heart is still beating. Lucky for me, it is. Unlucky for me, it is too. There's no way I'm imagining Zach's voice. I'd know it anywhere on any day of the week. My hand wraps around the silver knob, and I slowly turn the handle, trying to stay as quiet as possible, as if this is a horrible dream and once I open the door, I'll wake up. Except I know the possibility is moot. This is what horror movies are made of, like the leading character running upstairs instead of out the door when the killer is in the house. Well, look at me, staying rooted in place, opening a door to the scene in front of me. My best friend, or ex-best friend, is currently bent at the waist, maid of honor dress hiked up while my fiancé pistons his hips in and out of her body. Jesus, if this son of a biscuit eater isn't using a condom, I'm going to strangle him with my bare hands. Though, I'd bet my last dollar he isn't. Which means my wedding day, a day meant to be happy, is fucking toast. I mean, I'm not expecting it to be Cinderella magnificent, but this, this is the last thing I ever expected.

I could scream, I could cry, I could do both at once, but instead, I take a deep breath and open the door wider, allowing any passersby to get a bird's eye view of the free porn show, and I top it off even better: I clap. A standing ovation of one. It takes them a moment to realize I'm cheering them on. Mel and Zach stutter in their sexual escapades. "Bravo," I finally say. My hands come together in a rhythmic applause, repeating it until they get the idea they're no longer alone.

"It's not what it looks like." Zach pulls out of Melanie, sloppily, just as I figured. I'll be adding a doctor's appointment along with an STD testing. Yay fucking me.

"Are you fucking kidding me?" I'm calm, cool, and collected, almost too tranquil. My namesake is doing nothing for me right now because I should be angry and crying, yet none of those emotions hit me. I'm left feeling upset at myself more than anything. Did my friendship with Melissa mean so little that she'd toss

it away after more than twenty years of friendship, for sex with Zach? Zach, who I thought
was going to be my end all, be all. Boy, was I
wrong. Assuming really does make an ass out
of you and me.

"Stormy, please let us explain," Mel tries to
cajole me as if I'm one of her students at the
elementary school. I watch as she fixes her
dress, so at least I'm no longer seeing her
naked ass, and Zach's either. My eyes close, and
I breathe deeply, attempting to figure out what
to do next. How am I going to stand in front of
three hundred people, tell them the show is
over and they missed it in the groom's dressing
room?

"I don't think there's much to explain,
between Zach saying it's not what I think and
you wanting to explain." My eyebrows are
more than likely touching my hairline with
how tight my face feels. "What, did his dick fall
into your vag, or should we talk about how
you're so in love with a cheating dirtbag, you'd
willingly ruin everything to get what you
want?" I see the look in her eyes. This isn't a
quick fling. My idiot best friend is in love with
my fiancé. They are both stunned silent, Zach
looking everywhere but at me. The horrid
dress his mother insisted I wear, the venue she

chose, down to the flowers in the reception area, I did it for him, and now look where I am. This was never the wedding I envisioned, and Zach was never the man I was going to live with till the end of time.

"It's not like that. You have to believe me." Mel attempts to step toward me. My hand flies up, holding her back because there's no telling what I'll do if I have to smell the two of them on her body. It's one thing for the room to permeate the scent of sex; it's another to have it flaunted under your nose. Which I mean, isn't that what they've been doing all along? Zach remains silent. Thankfully, his tuxedo pants are zipped up, and I no longer have to see the evidence of their whatever this is.

"How long have you two been screwing each other behind my back?" I ask. Morbid curiosity creeps out of me. I'd like to say maybe I was part of the issue, but I know with every depth of my being it's not a me thing, it's a them thing. I witnessed this whole scenario play out with my parents in my teen years, a fourteen-year-old girl watching their dad walk out on them to start a new family with a new wife. It hits you bone fucking deep. Not once did my mom make me feel anything else than loved. She picked up the broken pieces of what she didn't leave behind while brushing herself off, waiting to cry at night when I was supposed to be asleep. The next morning, she'd wake up and do it all over again until one night, I didn't hear her cry. I heard her laugh at a television show, and that was when I realized my mom is stronger than any woman I've ever met.

"Stormy, what difference does it make?" My eyes narrow on Zach. His hands are in his pockets, tie is askew, hair a mess. The man in front of me isn't the man I thought I knew. My best friend, though, that's an even worse betrayal. Zach and Melissa have done the worst of the worst.

"Six months." Melissa clears her throat, forging on with the conversation. "We're in love, Stormy." I watch as my now former best friend moves closer to my now former fiancé, the two of them locking hands together, and that's all I can take. I need bleach for my eyes in a permanent kind of way. Someone needs to tell the guests what's going on, and I need three bottles of champagne, stat. I don't bother responding. My give a damn is busted. Those two lying, cheating scumbags deserve one another. While I was dealing with his nutcase of a mother wanting a perfect wedding for her, catering to her every whim while Zach was supposedly working well into the night and couldn't so much as help when I asked him to wade between his mother and me. It's why I'm in this stupid dress, at this stupid country club, with a stupid amount of people I didn't want in the first place. Obviously, Zach didn't either. He could have been a man about it, talked to me. I'd have at least been a bit more understanding. As it stands, I'm going to have to tell my mother, my aunt, and Zach's mother, Christine. Ugh, maybe I won't actually touch the subject with her. I know how that song and dance will go. She'll blame the entirety on me.

"Good luck. He told me that, too. I'm leaving. Figure this shit out on your own." I need to leave the room. There are no tears streaming down my face. That should be telling, right? I should at least be feeling a gamut of emotions. Except I'm not. I'm just done.

"It's different," Mel continues making a bad situation worse. An obnoxious cackle crawls up the back of my throat as my head rolls to the back of my neck. Apparently, everything is hitting me all at once—the wedding, dealing with Zach's awful mother, my own mother trying to smooth things over while still keeping the peace, absolutely hating how I've rolled over and taken the verbal abuse, and now this. Now freaking this. My chest tightens, my fingers tingle. Fuck, even my toes that are scrunched into a pair of too high heels are prickling. My hands go to my decolletage, nails scratching at the lace. I feel like I'm unable to drag enough air into my lungs. If this is what dying feels like, then please let there be white sandy beaches, the ocean air, the scent of my favorite coconut, pineapple, and sugar lotion on the other side. Those are my last thoughts as stars appear behind my closed eyelids. I'm unsure who closed them because I assure you I did not decide to feel like I'm this helpless person in front of Zach and Melissa. No way, no how, never ever. Yet that's exactly what happens. My whole body shuts down, and that's all she wrote.

Griffin

WORTHLESS PIECE OF SHIT. I was walking down the hall looking for the john when I stumbled upon my niece and what everyone knows is the groom looking disheveled. One plus one equals mother fucking two. On any given day, I'd keep to myself and walk the hell away. I've got enough drama in my life the way it is, running the local bar, dealing with waitresses, barbacks, and alcohol distributors, and that doesn't include the damn customers getting drunk off their asses, acting like damn idiots. That's not all I do either. Before I was a bar owner, I was a flight medic. Still am on the rare occasions there's a high-speed boat show nearby. This whole shindig isn't my idea of fun. If it weren't for the small town, my bar being the center of it, I wouldn't be here. Fucking appearances sake and keeping the gossip mongers off my damn back is part of the reason. The other is because of my niece, who's standing in front of me. Her best friend's wedding is today, and she needed a cash bar. Free publicity and flush pockets for a couple of bartenders—it was a no-brainer.

"Jesus, you two the reason for this?" Stormy, the bride, is currently in my arms, head lolled back, one of my arms bracketed beneath the back of her knees, the other beneath her neck. "Got nothing to say for yourselves?" I quirk an eyebrow at the two. Mel has the good sense to look away. Zach is too busy opening and closing his mouth, like a fish out of water, much like a bass once it's been caught and is trying to breathe. "Figures," I grumble. My eyes move from the pair of dumbasses to the woman in my arms.

I don't bother having a one-sided conversation. The way Stormy is, I'm willing to bet the two people in this room are the reason she's in the position she's in now. It doesn't matter that I'm walking away, carrying the bride out of this charade. Stormy leaving the groom and passed out from fainting, my, will the tongues wag. Fuck, she's lucky I stepped into the room. Lucky for us, no one is around when I walk out. The hallway is empty, and I'm trying to find a room that isn't cloaked with the scent sex, hoping Stormy doesn't come awake in my arms, do an about face, and hit me while doing so.

"Fuck," I grumble. My hand beneath her knees tries the doorknob, finding it locked. I set off for the next. The last thing she needs is attention in the state she's in. So, I head for the next door. This place has more rooms than a luxury hotel. The second doorknob twists open. I'm stepping inside, kicking the door shut with my foot. Locking it will have to wait. "Stormy, can you hear me?" I ask as I set her down on the couch.

"Ugh," she grumbles, eyes opening, a dazed look on her face when she notices it's me.

"You good?" She rolls over. I'm unsure of how to take that until she pulls it together enough to say, "Help. Off. I need to breathe." Her long dainty fingers are trying to pull on the buttons, scratching at the material.

"Son of a bitch." My hand knocks hers out of the way. I work at the buttons as fast as I can, and still, it's not fast enough for my liking, not with the way she's taking shallow needing to breathe. "Hold still, Stormy, don't move a fucking inch." I slide my hand inside my pants pocket, flip open my pocket knife, and flick the blade open. My eyes meet hers as she's looking over her shoulder. I'm willing to bet this contraption of a damn dress is the culprit for her collapsing in my arms all along.

"Hurry." With a steady hand I slice through the fabric, the knife cutting through echoes throughout what can be considered a gentleman's lounge. I was about to pull my cell phone out of my pocket to call an ambulance if she didn't wake up. Jesus, the way she came to, talking about her lack of breathing and pulling at her dress, two and two made four. Finally, the last button on her dress gives way, and she's taking a series of deep breaths. The damn thing was buttoned clear from her neck down to her lower back.

"Feel better?" I ask, trying not to notice the expanse of skin she's showing. I close my knife and place it back in my pocket. "Whoa, whoa, whoa, you think getting up that fast is smart?" My hands reach out, but I'm unsure of where to place them, yet damn if I'm not itching to feel her bare skin.

"I'm fine. I need to get out of here. Me and a bottle Jose Cuervo have a date, maybe more than one." She isn't listening to reason. I help her up, my hand going to hers, making sure she's steady on her feet before I let her go.

"Come on, I'll get you out of here. Plus, the saying goes, the best way to get over someone is to get under someone else." Stormy leans her body against mine. My arm moves to her lower back, where I meet her exposed skin, and Goddamn, does it feel good. She allows me to lead the way in her ripped dress, her hand holding the front in order for it not to slide down and give me a view I have no right wanting. Her hair is a mess, dark locks tumbling from the once upswept style. All I know is if anyone is going to make her forget today, it'll be me and my thick dick.

1

STORMY

Present Day

"Here goes nothing." It's been seven days, one hundred sixty-eight hours, ten thousand and eighty minutes since I walked out of my wedding venue with Griffin. I kept my head up, eyeing each and every passerby. They could think what they wanted. They did, by the way. The slew of nasty calls, texts, and voicemails that have been riddling my phone all week has not been my idea of fun. Zach's mom calling me every name under the sun. Clearly, her son hasn't fessed up to the reason of our demise. I get it. When Griff escorted me out, I was a hot fucking mess. Still, there's no need to call me a gold-digging slut. Then there was Mel's dad, God love him. Apparently, my ex-best friend fessed up to her shenanigans with my ex-fiancé, not all of the details but some. Funnily, her dad called, saying he'd hoped we'll eventually work our friendship out but if not he understood. Sadly, I'm not angry with him. It's Mel I'm upset with. I had to respond to Jack, letting him know that his family would still very much be a part of my life, but as for Mel and my friendship, it was over, so over, especially because she hijacked the honeymoon Zach and I went half and half on. Well, let's just say, a notification of a payment received for my half was also sent to my phone. At least I'm not losing more money as well as a vacation. The fucking douchebag and douchebagess are currently on what would be our honeymoon. As if I didn't want to get away from this damn town and run away.

Zach left without a backward glance, the same thing he obviously did with our relationship, only he's reaping a shit ton of rewards he doesn't deserve. Now, I'm here to thank a man who helped me when no one else could. A man who made inappropriate jokes to cheer me up while keeping me flush in the tequila while I got shit-faced drunk and passed out on his shoulder. I could have simply called or texted Griff, except I couldn't. Two days ago, my mom, Evelyn, and Aunt Catherine intercepted my cell phone. They noticed me picking up the colorful floral-incased phone, looking at it, and setting it facedown. Multiple times. By the fourth time, Aunt Catherine swooped in, read a few of the texts Zach's mom fired off, and confiscated the device. Between the man inside the double doors, my mom, and Aunt Catherine, they've been the light in this dark tunnel. When Zach left with Mel, he left me with everything. I had to make sure all the gifts we received were returned, as well as deal with the fallout of a few other things. You know, like my lease that's up in another month and how I'll be homeless since my landlord already has my place in a contract when I leave. My one saving grace is the two-week vacation I took from work. It's given me time to get shit in order, or not so in order, and hopefully, by the time I'm back to work, this small coastal town will have something else to talk about.

I pull the door open and take a step inside, the door closing behind me, secluding me in the dark bar. Cedar planks the walls and ceil-

ing. Beer and alcohol neon signs litter the walls
along with posters that look to be decades old.
My eyes take in the patrons lingering at the bar
and the high-top tables. A waitress is wiping
down the bar in my peripheral vision. She
gives me a slight nod. I do an awkward finger
wave. Great. More embarrassment floods my
body once again, adding fuel to the fire. My
mind tries to pull up the memory of my time
with Griff after he whisked me away from a
nightmare. I asked for his phone, made the call
to my mom. Between her and my aunt, they
helped put out the fires. Meanwhile, Griffin
had me loaded up, seatbelt secured, plopping
the bottles of tequila in my lap I pilfered on our
way, and we were driving. It's not like I stole
them; they were technically from my wedding,
which both parties helped pay for, myself
included, because while Mom did as much as
she could, there was no way we could keep up
with the Joneses and the way Zach's mom liked
to throw money out the window on frivolous
bullshit.

My gaze doesn't land on the man I came
here for. Maybe coming here was stupid.
Maybe I should leave well enough alone. Or
maybe I should pull up my big girl panties. My
voice of reason comes in loud and clear, which

means I'm going to listen and make my way to the bar. At least to ask the bartender where Griff is. If she says he's not here, then I can move on, write a thank-you card, and mail it to the bar I'm currently inside, aptly named High Tide Tavern.

I'm slightly underdressed compared to a few of the patrons. Most are in jeans, nice shirts, and boots. The tank top and cut-off jean shorts with a pair of flip-flops really don't mesh well with a bar. Open-toed shoes, beer bottles, and the possibility of a bar fight—my feet would be toast. Hopefully that doesn't happen, and I can come out unscathed. Plus, it's not like I'm here during last call. It's the early afternoon and in the middle of the week.

"Hi, welcome to High Tide Tavern. What can I get you?" the bartender asks after I finally shuffle my feet to the bar, where no one is sitting. She looks at me quizzically, as if I don't belong, a fact I'm very well aware of.

"Hi, actually, I was looking for Griff." Her eyebrows quirk up toward her hairline. She's got a slight smirk on her face as if she doesn't believe me.

"And you are?" Alright, then, maybe Griffin has women coming to his establishment asking for him all the time. Okay, fine, I can't technically blame them either. Griffin Hawkins is a lot of things. Ugly is not one of them. He's tall, dark, and devastatingly beautiful in a way most men would cringe at the term. Something tells me he wouldn't. Griff exudes confidence, a talent I wish I had. Maybe I wouldn't be standing here stone-cold silent trying to choose my words carefully.

"A friend, actually. Never mind, I'll see him when I see him." I shrug my shoulders. There's no way the bartender is going to tell me where Griff is or if he's even here. I'll cut my losses, send a thank-you card like the loser I am, and move on from another embarrassing moment in the life of Stormy Stevens. There's no reason to wait for a response. I abruptly close the conversation down. The bartender doesn't say anything else either and goes back to cleaning the countertops. That's when I turn around. There's no use sticking around, so I do what any other woman would do: I turn away, hold my shoulders back, and pretend to exude a confidence that's slowly crumbling. At least from the back it looks like I've got my shit together. From the front, well, that's a whole other story. My eyes are downcast, the dark circles rimming my eyes seem to be permanent these days, and my appetite is virtually nonexistent. It's been a domino effect: lack of sleep, lack of eating, lack of freaking energy. We'll just tack it on to everything else. Today, I'm going to hop in my car, roll the windows down, jack the air conditioner to the lowest setting, and find a good song to scream-sing to. I'm so lost in my own thoughts, trying to bolt toward the door without seeming like a basket case, I run smack dab into a hard body.

"If the world could just dig a hole and swallow me whole, that would be awesome right about now," I grumble into the black-fabric-covered chest, hands holding my biceps. The owner's scent wafts around us—orange, cedar, and oak.

"Baby girl," Griff's voice is rough with a raspy tone to it. As if he's smoked a cigarette or two. Only I know he doesn't. My eyes snap open, and trace the center of his chest until they meet his, which knocks me off my axis once again.

2

GRIFFIN

The softness in Stormy's eyes, the way her body shudders with the two words that slipped from my lips all too easily, fuck, it has me on fire. Clearly, that dumbass didn't make her feel like the woman she truly is or feed into her desires. What would have been her wedding night clued me in—you give the woman a bottle of tequila, and she lets lose real damn quick.

"Griff." Her eyes open after a beat. Cerulean blue, clear, and glassy, unlike the bloodshot eyes I had the pleasure of seeing while she popped off talking about how Zach couldn't even get her there. All I could do was grunt, bite back the words threatening to come out, and let her keep at it. She vented all while

taking another swig of tequila, not even
wincing as the strong alcohol slid down her
delicate throat. The woman can handle her
liquor, that's for sure. She tipped her head
back, my suit jacket draped over her shoulders,
and my eyes watched as it slid down. Fuck me,
I had no right to look at the glimpse of skin she
was giving me. Stormy's dress was destroyed;
there was no fixing it after I took my knife to it.
A knife that now sits inside a drawer in my
nightstand, one I no longer use. The way she
was sitting, I got the side profile of what I'm
sure is the sweetest set of tits a man could get
his eyes on. This woman should be off-limits.
I'm nobody's rebound, but it almost had me
throwing caution to the wind and say 'fuck it.'
Much like I am right now. Her body, my body,
on the nearest surface has my cock twitching.
The hard-on I've been walking around with for
days on end is more than ready and willing to
be let loose. I bet she's wet right now. The
woman gives off fuck-me vibes whenever I'm
near, and now is no different. The thought of
unbuttoning her jean shorts, sliding down the
zipper, the palm of my hand meeting her quivering stomach while moving down until my
fingers feel her softness. I'd bet her panties are
lace and see through, only adding to my inner

turmoil as the tips of my fingers hit the lips of her pussy. Now I'm wondering exactly what her cunt looks like. Are there soft curls, a landing strip, or is she completely bare? I'm going to find out, and fucking soon. It doesn't matter that we're in my bar. I'd do it in front of everybody to prove a point to Stormy. There's nothing wrong with her. She's just been with the wrong man all along. I'd work her until she was a quivering and moaning mess, not stopping until her body is wrung dry and she's holding on to me to stay standing. Somehow, I manage to keep my hands off the raven-haired beauty in front of me. An act of willpower and strength I usually retain for when I'm on a rescue mission with my crew when the high-speed boat races come to town or we head out of town if we're needed.

"You need something?" The last time I saw Stormy, she was toasted, dozing off on my shoulder on the beach, the discarded bottle of tequila near her feet, and I know it was time to call it a night. I carried her to my truck, got her settled in the passenger seat with her murmuring that she just wanted to feel, and it wasn't anything about emotions. Nope, Stormy left me speechless, talking about how she'd like to be fucked long and hard, hair pulled back as she's fucked from behind and experience an orgasm that Zach could never give her. I'm no damn saint. I thought about taking her up on the offer. That's also when I got another glimpse of her tits. Her dress dipped lower, and it took all I had to back the fuck away. She may not have said, 'Griff, take me to bed,' but with the vibes she was giving off, it was awfully tempting. I drove her home, carried her inside her apartment, and put her to bed. Stormy at least was cognizant enough to give me the code to her door, which pissed me off even more. What if I were someone else? Would she be just as willing?

"To talk to you." She raises her hands, and hovers them near my body, as if unsure if she should touch me out in the open where prying eyes can see. Newsflash, I don't give a flying fuck what people think. If Stormy wants to touch me, then goddamn, she can touch me any way she wants. I move a step closer, taking away the decision when her palms lie flat against my abdomen. My abs flex and her fingers clench into my muscles.

"Here or somewhere else?" I've heard the rumors, and noticed Stormy hasn't been out and about like she usually is. The random appearances she once made are gone. It didn't go unnoticed either that my niece and Zach aren't in town, adding fuel to the fire in the way of the rumor mill. The dust should have settled. It hasn't yet, and that's because of this small fucking coastal town, sinking its claws into gossip and not letting it go.

"It doesn't matter." The shrug of her shoulders says more than she's letting on. Christ, right now, there's a hesitance when she didn't have any the last time I saw her. It was also when I placed her in bed, her wedding dress sliding further off her body, and she didn't once think about using her hand to hold it up. I also realized she wasn't wearing a bra beneath, the fabric dipping so low I now know the color surrounding her nipples. The only reason I didn't take her up on her offer after she told me one too many times how she'd like to actually come with a cock inside her instead of a vibrating toy, was how inebriated she was. And believe me, it was fucking hard to hold back. Stormy's display of her tight body ended too fucking soon. She fell backwards, head hitting the pillow, arms spread wide, eyes closing, and was out like a damn light. The only sound in the room beside my heavy breathing was her soft sighs. There was nothing left for me to do. I wasn't going to stick around. She was far too much temptation, and if she woke up the next morning, forgetting about the whole night, yeah, I didn't even want to think about that. I went to her kitchen, grabbed a bottle of water, rummaged enough to find some pain reliever, and set it on her nightstand. My eyes landed on her one last time. She was out, hadn't even moved when I put the blanket on top of her. My fingers grazed her collarbone, and I knew it was now or never. I walked out of her apartment like the fires of hell were on my heels and I couldn't trust myself to do something too fucking dangerous. I hit the button on her keypad, heard the deadbolt click into place, tested the knob, and haven't seen her since. Until today.

"Barbie!" I call out to my lead bartender, the one who runs the bar when I'm out for a couple of days every now and then.

"Yeah, Griff?" she responds without looking up from pouring a beer from the tap.

"You good for a bit?" I came in early to work on some paperwork and relieve her when I was through.

"As long as I'm off by five, I'm good." She glances up after placing the glass in front of Rodger, one of the old timers who comes here every day after he's off his shift.

"Appreciate it." Stormy's hands cling to my stomach still. She doesn't look over her shoulder or anywhere else besides my chest.

"No problem," she replies. My hand finally goes to Stormy's, holding them to my chest as I take a step backward, opening the bar door with my back.

"Come on, we'll hit the beach." She nods, loosening her hold on me when the sun hits us. She squints her eyes, and I take my sunglasses off the neck of my shirt, handing them to her, and pull my hat down lower to shield my own.

"Thanks. I won't take too much of your time." Our bodies gravitate toward one another, my hand going to her lower back as she puts my sunglasses on.

"I've got plenty of time for you, Stormy." She doesn't stutter in her steps, but I do hear her quick intake of breath, and a grin takes over my face. It seems she likes that I speak my mind, a damn good thing, too, because I'll be telling her exactly what I want once we're down by the beach.

3

STORMY

aby girl. I'm not dreaming, right? Those two words currently have a chokehold on me, and I'm dissecting them internally. Maybe he uses that for every woman he's around, or maybe he doesn't. The doesn't part of this scenario has me thinking it's for me only, especially when Griff stepped closer to me, and I felt something. Okay, fine, it wasn't something; it was *everything*. Everything Zach was not—long, thick, and unbelievably hard. Maybe throwing myself at him when I was drunk didn't backfire on me after all.

Griff's bar, High Tide Tavern, is on the beach, a small boardwalk. I'm kicking off my sandals, allowing the hot sand to sink between my toes, the hot sun beating against my shoulders. The salty breeze causes a few tendrils of hair to come loose from of my ponytail and blow across my face.

"So," I say to break the silence, turning to face Griff instead of watching the waves crash against the shore. He waits until I'm ready to keep going. I'm noticing more and more he's the strong silent type. He's also a man who takes care of you when you can't take care of yourself. Water, Tylenol, and a scrawled note saying, 'Drink this, take the meds, Griff.' That was all, but it was substantial in a way that his note is tucked away in the bottom of my nightstand drawer. "I didn't," I start to say when Griff's hand comes up, fingers brushing against my cheek, moving the tendrils of hair that are currently stuck to my lips away. I lose my train of thought. I lose every piece of me when Griff is near, the way his scent surrounds me the closer we get. It clung to his suit jacket, and it took everything I had not to bring it to my nose while wearing it and inhaling the scent deeply.

"What were you saying?" His honey-gold eyes hold mine captive. His sunglasses make it easy for me to stare at him without him realizing, hopefully. It's probably wishful thinking, though. And what does this man do? The unexpected. His hand stays where it is, thumb holding my hair back, while the rest of his fingers are holding my hair back, gently massaging my scalp. Maybe it's a good idea for his borrowed sunglasses. Griff can't see my eyes closing, but I'm sure he can hear the sigh that leaves my mouth. This week has been hard. I've done everything I can to make sure things were taken care of. The only bad part that's not in this whole scenario is where I'm supposed to live. I was that girl. My lease was almost up, so I let my landlord know I'd be moving out. Zach's place was bigger than mine, and it made sense to move in with him. Boy, was I wrong. Now, I've got a week to vacate my place, and it's filled with more boxes than I care to admit. My obsession with poetry books is crazy, even I can admit that, the older the better. I refuse to part with them or downsize my collection. The warning signs were there, red flag after red flag, not a beige one in sight. Yet I still didn't see him and Mel together.

"Well, I... uh, never got to say thank you for taking care of me. I know that wouldn't be anyone's idea of a great way to spend a Saturday night. I'm just, well, really thankful."

My eyes are finally open, watching to see what he'll do with the words I gave him. I made a complete ass out of myself, talking about the lack of orgasms Zach was able to manage to give me, and I'm pretty sure I threw my arms around his body, nuzzled his neck, not to mention my tongue snuck a taste of the column of his throat. Yeah, tequila definitely lowers my inhibitions. What it doesn't do is allow me to lose my memory. Another traitorous bitch I need to quit. Tequila, a best friend named Melissa, and an ex-fiancé. Though sadly, I'm still tied to the dickface until I get everything figured out, but that will have to wait. He's on what would be our honeymoon, and me, well, maybe I'm not much better. Because Griffin is right here in front of me, and the only thing I can think about is how it would feel to be beneath him.

"Stormy, I give you any reason that I wasn't where I wanted to be?" His question brokers no room for argument. It's gruff but not in a stern way. In a way that leaves no discussion necessary, which is hard for me to swallow because I've yet to show him how appreciative I am.

"No. That still doesn't mean a person can't say thank you." I start to take a step back, but he clearly doesn't like that idea. The hand cupping my cheek, so to speak, pulls me into his body. We're close, too close and if we want to keep the gossip out of the tongue wagers mouths we should back away from one another, except we don't.

"You said it. It's over and done." He leaves it at that, making me think this is a bad idea. It couldn't be all in my head. The man is basically marking his territory right now and earlier at the bar.

"Well, okay. I guess that's all." There's no need to stick around once I've said thank you. I mean, sure, I could have baked him cookies or offered to take him out to dinner, but life is a bitch. My kitchen is packed and, well, any extra spending is not happening while I figure out where I'm moving in a week. Does anyone know how hard it is to find a place to live in seven days? I do. It's near impossible, and the longer I procrastinate, the worse it gets. My mom said I could move in with her. Sure, it wouldn't be for long, just until an apartment became available in my current complex or another that would be in my budget. It's all a pain in the ass to deal with since I'm a hair stylist. We get paid differently, and it's a nightmare to get that ready to submit to a bank or rental company. If I were to take my mom up on her offer, well, that would also mean living with my fun, crazy, never-stops-moving aunt. I love her, I do, but I also like the quiet, and there won't be a lot of that should I move in with them.

"That's not all," Griff says after a few moments of silence. Silence that has me on edge with worry. I tilt my head to the side, waiting him out. Unsure of what he's going to say next, worried really because if that's not all, is he going to bring up my craziness when I was drowning myself in tequila?

"It's not?"

"Nope. How much do you remember of that night?" Fuck me sideways. Of course he'd bring that up.

"All of it," I admit after *wishin' and hoping, and thinkin' and prayin'* he wouldn't ask that. Yes, I'm singing that song in my head while reciting the lyrics. I mentioned my aunt was crazy, right? Well, it seems some of her crazy was passed down to me. Responding in song lyrics is not part of our thing.

"Good, then this won't come as a surprise. That ride you were willing to go after, you'll get it from me and no one else." My mouth opens and closes as I gulp for air like a fish out of water. No one has ever been so blatant to me about sex, though I wasn't really quiet either. Zach was my first and last, which obviously was lackluster at best. Stupid me, marrying a man at the age of twenty-four who would get his rocks off and leave me in another form of denial. Thankfully, I was a pro at self-satisfaction. And Griff now knows all there is about that subject as well.

"Umm..." I'm still at a loss for words. God, I'm an idiot.

"You got any plans for this evening?" I shake my head no, wondering what he is after.

"Good, I'm at the bar tonight. I'll be closing it down, or I'd take you to dinner like a man should. That being said, we'll have dinner there tonight."

"Um, Griff, you don't have to do that. You're working and, well, shouldn't it be me paying or offering dinner to you?" I reply with trepidation in my voice.

"Baby girl, we're having dinner tonight. You want to cook dinner for me, I'll take it, but you are not paying." Well, okay, then, growly alpha man has entered the chat.

"I mean I can't cook for you, not that I can't cook, but, well, you saw my apartment. Everything is packed up." Griff looks at me like I've got two heads. The verbal vomit is a real thing when I'm confused and worried and, well, all the things really.

"Dinner at the bar it is, then." His hand

slides down my neck, squeezing the tight muscles once. I hold back a moan, barely. His hand continues its downward path. My body lights up beneath, and a tremble runs through me.

"Okay." There's a slight tilt to his lips as his hand wraps around mine, holding my hand firmly in his, and then he's leading us back up the dock. I'm left in a Griff-induced stupor, not completely sure what just happened, yet I like it all the same.

4

GRIFFIN

"I hope you know what you're doing." Barbie doesn't mince words. Her voice is quiet yet speaks volumes. She's been with me from the very beginning of opening the bar. It's why I'd ever allow her to question what I'm doing. If it were anyone else speaking to me like that, well, they'd have fewer fucking teeth. That being said, this is Barbie. She's got a past of her own in this small town, except the rumors swirling around her were no fault of her own. Her parents were the talk of the entire town at one point. The epitome of toxic, one a drunk, the other an addict. It's a wonder Barbie came out unscathed. That doesn't mean a part of her isn't hardened. She has a few times a year where she'll allow herself a moment to grieve when she lets those walls down. Both her parents are gone due to a car crash a few years back. One or both were intoxicated and had a fight that the whole town square could hear. When the news was delivered that they were killed after going double the speed limit on the highway, lost control, and did a lot of flips, Barbie was on shift. A small hint of emotion took over but also a look of relief. So, her bringing it up, completely valid. Shit, I've been doing exactly that since the night I was with Stormy. So many worries, issues, and hurdles we'll have to jump through in order to get to where we're going. I take my baseball cap off my head, run my fingers through my hair, and leave it off since I'm inside the bar and the sun isn't blaring in my eyes. I contemplate what Barbie said again, choosing my words carefully before I respond. My head is in the damn clouds, consumed with the way Stormy felt against me, how she gave in to my touch so freely. The soft sigh she tried to hide still replays in my mind. The only thing that could have made it better is if she was moaning my damn name.

"You and me both." Staying vague while I've got my head in the fucking clouds might be the best plan of action. The less Barbie sees, the less shit she'll give. The last thing I need to do before work is hashing this out with her. It's Saturday night, which means it'll be a full fucking house. As it is now, I'm going to need Nav, my barback, to help even more. My nighttime bartender, Jeremy, can handle everything else in order for me to get inventory done for the liquor and beer distributor.

"Talk about jumping from the frying pan into the fire." Fucking Barbie. I take a deep breath, give her my back, and grab the clipboard off the side of the shelf that holds the liquor. I'm not sure what she thinks talking about this will do. I've made my decision. It seems Stormy has as well, or she wouldn't have agreed to come back up after thanking me. Christ, all the thanks I needed was the glimpse of her tits when she was drunk, and we could have called it even. Now it seems like I'm going to get way more than a view.

"Listen, you've said your piece. I've got a lot of love for you, but this, it's not up for discussion, Barbie. You wanna be my eyes and ears, I'll take that. This damn town won't be nice, no matter what." Not to Stormy at least. She's in a vulnerable place right now, and everyone has noticed that she's not been coming and going like she did before shit went down.

"Message received, loud and clear, but all bets are off if your brother comes in." I chuckle. Barbie and my older brother, Jack, are like fire and ice. It's been a long time since Jack and I have seen eye to eye. I'm the blue-collar brother, working as a rescue medic. Where he's white collar, who wears a suit and tie to the office daily. I started out as soon as I graduated high school, worked for the local department here in Jasmine, South Carolina. As time went on, I knew staying where I was wouldn't mean making the kind of money I am now. So, I worked my ass off, picked up extra shifts working the boat races up and down the east coast as a rescue medic. Then I came back home, and set up High Tide Tavern. I still work at the boat races, and that's where Barbie comes in. She's a magician behind the bar and keeps shit running smoothly while I'm out of town. Now, when Jack comes in, the same can't be said. He likes to piss her off, she likes to give him hell, and I fucking hear the stories when I'm back home.

"I'll deal with Jack. I should probably stop by his house tomorrow," I grunt, tossing the clipboard and pen down on the bar. "Get out of here. You've got better things to do than to hang out here all weekend." She takes off her apron, starts shutting down her register, and going through the tip jar.

"You better, and I'm leaving. I can't wait to have the next two days off. I'm going to turn off all my devices, hit the beach, and sleep." Barbie is younger than me, not by a lot, and definitely older than Stormy. Fuck, that adds even more. Stormy is twenty-four, rebounding from that dick bag while also dealing with the fallout of her best friend committing a betrayal. Then there's me, thirty-nine, a bar owner who has never settled down. And who am I dead set on going after? Stormy, my niece's ex-best friend.

"Be safe. Next weekend, you good to cover? I'll work the days leading up if you and Jeremy can take over Friday through Sunday." I'm sure she saw the schedule I hung in the employee break room. I'm not that much of an asshole that I'd assume Barbie would see it without saying anything.

"Yep, just make sure we're stocked, and I'll handle the rest." This is why I won't piss her off too much. She will take care of everything except dealing with distributors. I get it. She's making great money, but not enough to deal with assholes who like to stock it on top of the old stuff, leaving us with skanky beer if Nav or I am not here.

"You got it." Another hour or so, and the two old timers who are at the other end of the bar will cash out. There'll be another lull for an hour before the after-dinner crowd comes in. Saturday night is a different animal. At least it's not Thursday, when the college kids come in, drink so much they act like fucking idiots, start fights, and I have to either clean up a mess or call the cops.

"See you later." Barbie finishes up and then heads toward the employee area. I get back to looking over the bottles, checking which ones need to be replaced before I head to the storage area to restock and figure out what we need. The best thing I did was make this a true bar. No food means one less thing to deal with. The downside is too much alcohol in a person's body without food, fuck, it makes for a nasty cleanup at times.

"Later. You want me to walk you out?" I ask, already aware of the answer. Barbie has yet to take me up on my offer, but come next weekend, Nav will escort her out when they close down. She knows if not, I'll fire her ass.

"No, I'm good. Get to work, slacker." I don't look up from what I'm doing. It doesn't matter if I did; she'd be gone, leaving me with two patrons. The only reason we open early is for our regulars. When they quit coming, I'll re-evaluate our operating hours. Until then, we'll keep on keepin' on.

5

STORMY

"Ugh, this is impossible." I'm sitting on the floor in my living room, laptop on the coffee table while pouring over the Internet in search of a place that has availability within the next few days. I swear the same ones keep popping up; I get excited only to realize I've already called them when my mom and aunt were here yesterday, the phone still commandeered. Today is the last day, literally. If I can't find anything to move into by Wednesday at the latest, I'll be screwed. Which means I'll be finding a storage unit and have to move in with my mom. No one wants to move back home after being out on their own for so long. And while my mom and aunt are super chill, it's still a piece of my independence that will be sliced through. Kind of like a big, fat failure on your forehead, you know, like the one on mine right now. Except this godforsaken town is pinning it all on me. Let's just continue doing the same for the remainder of this shitty-ass month.

It also doesn't help matters that my whole way home, I was anywhere but where I needed to be. My mind was on a certain man, you know, the man I shouldn't want, the man who makes me feel something. And I still have his sunglasses. I guess I'll give those back to him in a couple of hours when I see him. Griff created a whole slew of nerves that are swirling through my nervous system, a buildup of what could happen—not *could* happen, *would* happen, especially because I'd fling myself at him to feel like the woman I know I am. The one who I allowed Zach to staunch. Before my ex-fiancé, I had a few boyfriends, dabbled in various activities, just not sex. I gave my virginity to him, stayed with him, and never once got off with his hands, mouth, or cock. The past boyfriends could at least make me feel desired. So, yeah, it's been years since I've felt the way Griff makes me feel. He makes me feel alive.

"Get your shit together, Stormy," I mutter

under my breath, ready to slam my laptop lid closed. If my vibrator weren't already packed, I'd go to my room and use the life-like dick to relieve the ache between my legs. The need to unpack it sits close to the surface. I won't, though, not yet at least. Will I probably tonight when I come back home? Absolutely, especially if Griff teases me. The way he was adamant about him being the one to make my first orgasm with a man happen. My body trembles wondering how he plans on doing so. Will he use his fingers, his mouth, a combination of both or will he say screw it, and take me with his cock. I want to know how he'll do it, and I want it to be him. My thighs clench once again, clit throbbing, a permanent state of being whenever I think of Griff. The need to be with a real man is at an all-time high.

I click on a new link, finding a website that I've yet to see, and man, does it have potential. A two-bedroom, one-bath, close to the salon. A little over what I want to spend, but I can always open my books, take on a few new clients, and be okay. "Please let this work out," I pray to the apartment gods, fingers crossed, ready to do whatever I can to make this happen. Seven days is not enough time, and had I not been in this self-imposed shelter staying away from everyone and everything, this could have been done a lot faster.

"Knock-knock, Stormy, Stormy," Aunt Cat, short for Dorothy, says on the other side of the wall, not even bothering to knock. I scramble up from my place on the floor and head to unlock the door before she uses her key. You know, the one that's supposed to be used for emergencies only. They've both done that before. One time I was in the shower, I didn't answer when they stopped by, and I nearly had a heart attack. There is nothing quite like stepping out of the shower and coming face to face with what you think is an intruder only for it to be your mom. The screaming commenced, and with Aunt Cat rounding the corner, it happened all over again.

"Coming, Aunt Cat!" Luckily, this apartment is small, so in a few short steps, I'm at the door, unlatching the deadbolt and flinging the door open. There, standing beside my aunt, is my mother. Aunt Cat has a smile plastered on her face, arms full of paperwork, and I'm dreading it. They left yesterday with the promise to return today. The timing couldn't be worse, and yet it couldn't be better.

"Hey, honey," Mom says as I open the door further, allowing them access. Aunt Cat kisses my cheek, and Mom brings me in for a hug. "Hey, Momma, did you by chance bring my phone back? I think I found a place, but calling would be easier than emailing."

"I did. Aunt Cat blocked a slew of people, so you should be good from those who shall not be named. I figured a week without a phone would be plenty of time." We pull away from one another, and I nod. It's time to get with the program and start getting out and about again. The rumors are going to circulate no matter what. I'm tired of hiding from the whispers.

"Thank God. Do I want to know what all that paperwork is?" I ask, a different kind of nerves taking over. There's so much left unfinished. Though I did make calls to see what would happen money wise earlier this week, a lot of the vendors had to get back with me. Deposits would for sure be lost; it's the getting socked with the full amount of the reception that would cripple me. Zach's mom wanted the venue at the country club. So, the least she can do is pay for the reception; the deposit is on Mom. So, I'll pay that back and deal with the ceremony another day. I'll be paying that for the next forty years. Sadly, Mom is stuck with the cost of my dress and shoes unless I repay her, which I will if my bank account allows it. That's an inconvenience but nothing compared to the embarrassment. When Zach and Melissa come back, it'll kick back up again, so wonderful of them, too.

"You'll want to know about it. My sister, your aunt, has a way of finagling companies. She's getting you a lot of the money back in exchange for not having to deal with Zach's mother." My mother, Evy, short for Evelyn, does a disgusted roll of her shoulders at the mention of Zach's mother, Laura. The feeling is entirely mutual. Another red flag I woefully ignored.

"Okay, let me make this call, and then we'll get to it. I'd love to be able to get some of your money back, and if I can't, you know I'll repay you," I tell my mom as she hands me the phone. I don't bother looking at my screen in case there are more harassing texts and calls.

"That's enough. You will not pay me back because you dodged a bullet. The proudest moment of my life." I arch an eyebrow, cross my arms overs my chest, and really look at her. "Okay, fine. Besides you being born and going through all the milestones. The last thing you need is a man like that. Honey, there are way better men out there."

"And she's found zero of them, but from what I hear, you and Griff are burning the town down with the smolders he's throwing your way," Aunt Cat interjects, setting down the stack of papers on the counter before pulling out a barstool and waving us over.

"As if you have much room to talk, Cat." This is their normal way of talking to one another; it's been like this since I moved out of my mom's house and Aunt Cat moved in. I love that they have one another, but sometimes the antics can be too much, especially if I had to live with them twenty-four hours a day, seven days a week.

"Alright, I'm going to make a phone call. So, you two, pipe down." I give them both a pointed look, and they have the nerve to give me an innocent face. I'm on a mission and head toward the small covered patio, hopeful for some good news.

6

GRIFFIN

"Keep your eyes to your fuckin' self." I slap the back of Nav's head when Stormy walks in. The fool can't even keep his tongue inside his mouth. Shit, neither can half the damn bar. Men and women alike are looking at Stormy, a smoke show of a woman. I watch as their eyes rove from her face to her tits, down her sexy-as-fuck legs, and when she walks by, their eyes are locked on her ass.

"Ah, shit, had no idea. You know what they're saying about her, right?" Nav asks, eyes no longer on Stormy but on me. My own gaze is locked on the woman of the hour, so I only notice Nav isn't looking at her anymore in my peripheral view.

"Nav, shut the fuck up. You and Jeremy are on tonight. I'll have my walkie talkie on, but don't use it unless it gets too rowdy." I don't hear him respond or stick around. Tourist season is winding down. Things shouldn't get too bad, and I'll step in if need be. After Barbie left, it was quiet enough for me to place an order for sandwiches, chips, and fruit. I didn't have a clue what Stormy liked besides tequila. Pretty sure her liver would revolt if I brought out the preferred Patron she drinks. Club sandwiches were the easiest thing I could think of, and it'd be easier for her to dissect if needed. Once the guys came in, I went into the office to put in the beer and liquor order. The last thing I need to before I head out next Thursday is make sure paper and plastic products are stocked in the supply closet.

"Message received, loud and clear," I hear Nav say to my back. The crowd parts, allowing me to easily navigate. A few nod their heads, some say hello. I ignore all of them. I'm on a one-track mission for Stormy, who is standing near the door, her eyes searching for me. A sweet smile softens her face when she finds me. Gone is her frown. Stormy's wearing a black tight-fitting top with not even a hint of cleavage, but these fuckers have no problem salivating at wanting a taste. Too fucking bad. They'll never get that ride they're after. Her short jean skirt is tight around her hips, showing off legs that were made to be wrapped around my head or waist. My mouth waters yet again. I tuck my tongue inside my cheek to hold off any wayward thoughts that would have my cock thicken in length. Clearly, the head between my legs isn't willing to sit down and shut up. A vision of Stormy with that sinful skirt around her waist, legs spread open while she's in my lap assaults my mind. Her top pulled up, bra beneath her tits holding them up for me to wrap my mouth around her taut nipples, one right after the other. Jesus, this woman has my dick wrapped in knots.

"Hey." I can barely hear her over the music playing through the speakers, the bass vibrating off the walls as well as the stomping of feet on the dance floor.

My head descends, mouth going to her ear and whispering, "Baby girl." Her hands come to my sides, hands clenching the fabric of my shirt, white and emblazoned with High Tide Tavern in bold black letters, my uniform in case I'm needed. When Stormy saw me earlier, the shirt I was wearing was grey, stained, and soaked with sweat after working outside. A complaint came in about the lights in the parking lot not working. The last thing I want is for someone to leave the bar at two o'clock in the morning and not feel safe.

"Griff." She leans into me, digging into my sides. The need to get us away from the doorway in case a person comes barreling inside and slams into her drives me.

"Come on." My teeth nip at her earlobe before I pull away, maneuvering us so I'm now beside her and my hand is on her lower back. What I don't expect is Stormy to loop her arm around me in a similar fashion or for her thumb to slide into my belt loop. There are a few looks tossed our way as I we walk toward the back of the bar. "Hey, Griff, good to see you," a customer says. His hand is out, and fuck it all to hell, I can't necessarily do nothing. They're paying customers, the reason I'm able to breathe easier and not have to work as many shifts as I once did.

"Hey, man, good to see you, too." My right hand takes his. Unfortunately, it causes me to lose my hold on Stormy's waist. It's quick with one man, then it turns into another asking, "Hey, you plan on expanding anytime soon? I've got a friend who retired and is looking to sell his bar in the town over." Talking shop isn't what I want to do right now, and adding another bar to my already hectic schedule is even less.

"I haven't thought about it, honestly. I'm pretty set right now, but be sure to leave the information with Jeremy at the bar, and I'll take a look," I reply.

"Will do," he responds.

"Have a good night." I close down any further conversations with others. Stormy's here because I asked her to come, not to watch me work. It was me who was unwilling to wait until tomorrow when the bar is closed and we could have some damn alone time. If I weren't hellbent on being around her as much as possible now that she opened the door, I would have waited. It's no longer an option. Stormy is doing shit to me I never thought possible. Thinking things like giving up my adrenaline junkie ways in order to be home more. Yeah, there's a lot standing in our way, but who fucking cares? I sure don't, and the town of Jasmine, South Carolina better get it out of their heads that they'll make her feel uncomfortable.

"You okay?" Stormy's once relaxed body is now rigid. No longer is she leaning toward me, and her hand that was holding me is now gone.

I was so caught up in trying to shut a conversation down that I didn't realize something had happened. My eyes sweep over her face, cataloguing her look, noticing she's looking straight ahead, at the dance floor yet not. She is closing down. Something happened, and I want to know the who, what, and why. Now.

"Yep, I'm fine." Clearly, she's not fine. It's the furthest from the truth, but talking about it out in the open with more prying eyes is not what she needs.

"Come on." My hand resumes its place on her lower back, and I notice hers doesn't. This time, the crowd doesn't clear as much of a path. More people are piling in, and my only option is to move Stormy so she's in front of me. The scowl on my face must show people I'm busy because no one stops us again as we forge a path on the outside of the dance floor. The lights go from shining in different colors to a more muted tone. We finally hit the door to the employee only hallway. I punch in the code, open the door, and the noise quiets down once it shuts behind us.

"Wow, I had no idea how this was set up," Stormy says. My hand reaches for hers as we walk toward my office.

"Working is impossible when you can't

hear yourself think. This is all soundproof. The main door has a keypad, and so does my office." I'm behind her and her hand on the railing, hips swaying and jean skirt hiking up a sliver at a time.

"That makes sense." I count each step. My cock is ready to take things farther. My head is telling me to calm the fuck down and figure out what had Stormy upset downstairs. The damn bastard, he doesn't like that idea. Well, that's too damn bad.

"Put the code in, Seven-Four-Seven-Zero," I give her the code to my office, hands going to her hip and my front plastered to her back.

"Griff." Her voice trembles as she does what I say, no questions asked.

"We're going to talk, mainly you. I want to know what happened downstairs, then we're going to eat. If this night plays out like it should, you'll be in my bed. Tonight." She turns around, hair swinging around her shoulders as she does, and I step into her space. I watch as her eyes heat with desire, then narrow into slits, and finally, she takes a deep breath and holds it for a moment, as if she's counting to five in her head before letting it out.

"Let it go. It doesn't matter. And who said anything about me sleeping with you?" She cocks a hip, a tilt of a smile tugging at the corner of her lips.

"Not letting it go. If I have to get it out of you another way, I will, and baby girl, no one said a word about sleeping tonight." Her sharp intake of breath is the only tell I need. My hands grip her waist, pulling her toward me, my legs bracketing her on either side as she walks backwards, not stopping until my desk meets her ass, and then my mouth is on hers.

7

STORMY

Griff takes my mouth, that's the only way to describe it. There's no buildup, no soft touches or slow licks. My hair is fisted, he's holding me where he wants, lips and tongue devouring me whole, and I'm along for the ride, eagerly. If Griff were to hold me captive, I'd be his willing victim. If only I could keep hold of this feeling. The sensations are unlike any I have ever experienced before, Zach and with the others. No one has ever me feel alive. It's as if I'm on a tightrope, balancing for dear life, holding on as tightly as I can but letting go. It would be the most freeing ever.

"Griff." I pull away for a moment. He clearly doesn't like that even if it is to catch my breath. His teeth nip at my lower lip, pulling me back into his intoxicating vortex. He doesn't respond. I wasn't expecting an answer. I also wasn't expecting to have a kiss rock me to my core. My head tips back, giving his mouth access to travel to my chin, nipping at it much like he did my lips, tongue lapping at it to soothe away any pain he may have caused. Newsflash, I like the way he bites me and the moan that lives me only spurs him on further.

"Fuck, yeah," Griff mutters along the column of my neck. He stops at the pulse point. My core tightens with each pull, body arching to get closer to him. My hands are tangled in his shirt, pulling the fabric up with the tips of my fingers until I finally meet his skin. Griff bites at my neck, no doubt leaving a mark of some kind, a brand if you will. One that I'm sure can and will be seen by the town of Jasmine, and I will absolutely not cover it up. It'll be my badge of honor for finally finding a piece of myself I thought was broken. His hand tightens its hold in my hair. "I want you to watch. Keep your eyes focused on what I'm doing, Stormy." I feel his hand on the outside of my thigh, more skin pressing against skin. The fire inside me is building rapidly with each firm touch of his body. Griff pulls up my skirt with deft fingers until he can't any longer. My eyes move to his face and then to what he's doing to my body. He's dominating my mind, my senses, and my body. It's soul consuming. I want to bare it all. Give everything to him and let him take control.

"Lift up, baby girl. Let me see you." His thumb sweeps up the inside of my thigh, edging dangerously close to my pussy. The body suit I'm wearing is the only thing between his hands and my bareness. One snap of the metal clasp between my legs, and Griff would see it all.

"Oh God." I lose my hold on his body in order to do what he said, hands pressing down on his desk to lift my ass off the dark wood desk. Griff slides my skirt up even higher until it's wrapped around my waist. Never once when I got dressed before I walked over to Griff's bar did I think this is where I would land —on his desk, spread open, him working me into such a fevered pace that I feel like one small brush along my clit would make me explode.

"I'm not God, baby girl, but I am your daddy." My eyes find his face. Another wave of shock rolls through my body, and it's not in disgust. It's in pure unadulterated lust. The

look I give Griff must be more than enough
answer that I'm okay with him calling himself
that or for me to use it. My hands that were on
the desk take ahold of his shirt, trying to pull it
off his body. If I'm going to be half naked, he
can be, too. He gets the memo. His hand in my
hair disappears, and holy fucking shit, I watch
as he grabs at the neck of his shirt from behind
and pulls it up and over his head. My gaze is
glued to each delicious inch of skin he uncov-
ers. He doesn't' have a stomach that's the
perfect eight-pack most girls and women want;
it's lightly muscled with some softness. My
hands reach out to feel more of him, hovering
over his abdomen, and when he steps closer,
the tips of my fingers trace a tattoo on his
ribcage. I watch as his body locks up, and it's
good to know I'm not the only one affected in
this situation. His left arm is covered in tattoos,
a sleeve devoid of any color. Waves give way to
a serpent, carrying it to the back of his hand. I
mean, sure, I've seen his lower arm and hand,
but nothing prepared me for the full effect of
Daddy Griff.

"You're gorgeous," I pause. "Daddy." The
words slip out of my mouth. Griff responds by
taking a step closer. We're meshed together.
Fused, so to speak, his hard, thick, and what

appears to be long dick throbbing against my aching center.

"Christ, baby girl. You good with this?" he asks, circling his hips, his bulge hitting my clit again. I nod in response. Words are harder to formulate as he continues his ministration. My head rolls back on my shoulders, eyes closing, and a long moan is all I can force to come out. "I need words, Stormy, or this stops." I'd like to see him try. I'm so close to coming, and should he stop, well, I'm not sure if I would survive. I'd probably take matters into my own hands, push him until he's planted in the chair he has in front of his desk. My fingers would attack his belt, button, and zipper until I could finally get my hands wrapped around his cock. A quick pull on my bodysuit would have it open, and I could sink down on him until he'd be planted deeply inside me.

"Stormy," he grunts, getting my attention. Both of his hands tighten on the cheeks of my ass, the tips of his fingers pressing in further. What I don't expect is for him to grasp the thong part of the bodysuit that's attached and pull on it. My eyes pop open, head comes forward, and I mewl at the sensation. Griff might be asking a question, one he already knows the answer to, but it's not stopping him from making me fall apart. "Answer me, or I'm stopping." His thumb sweeps beneath the black fabric, right at the entrance to my pussy, while the other keeps working the front patch of my bodysuit to rub against my clit.

"Don't stop. Please don't stop." It's not an answer because the only thing I can think about is chasing a high, a high so tall and big that I'm dying to crash over. It's as if my body is in the ocean, feet spread part, as I watch as the wave rolling closer, bracing for impact, and still, once it hits you, you're not prepared. That is the exact feeling that's overwhelming me right now.

"Mouth, baby girl, now." Griff's voice comes out harsh. There's no brokering his demand, and that's exactly what it is. It's not a request, it's a command, one I follow without pause. He takes over our kiss before it even begins while keeping up his ministrations on my clit. His thumb slides inside my pussy, and I pulse around him, my body greedy for the orgasm I'm finally going to successfully achieve without using my own fingers or toys. It's never felt this good. Ever. His teeth nip at my lips, tongue lapping, and then he's diving full steam ahead. His teeth nip at my lips, tongue lapping, and then he's diving full steam ahead. Just like everything else with the man standing in front of me, he takes over in the best way possible.

"Please," I breathe into his mouth, wanting more of his fingers inside me, wanting to feel the stinging burn when he pushes me to my limits with his thick fingers.

"More what?" Griff pulls on my bodysuit, using it as a seesaw, unbothered by the fact I'm sure it's going to be destroyed. I'm going to keep it forever, look at it hanging in my closet as one of the greatest moments of all times.

"More." I bear down on his thumb. "More everything." My hands slide up until I'm using his shoulders for leverage to lift up, showing Griffin what I want, and when he pulls his thumb out of my pussy, I mewl, "Daddy," leaving me feeling unfulfilled. Until his thumb leaving becomes two fingers. There's no buildup, not that I need it. The sound of my wetness clues me in to the fact along with our labored breathing.

"Fuck, yeah, baby girl. Keep at it. Show daddy how hard you can come." Jesus Christ, my body trembles with Griff surrounding me. This man does not shy away; if anything, he pushes me farther than ever. He adds another finger. My pussy has a tight chokehold on his finger, the way he's working my clit with my clothes. A wetness like I've never felt before rushes out of me. I have no idea what it is or if it's okay. All I know is it takes over and leaves me feeling incredible.

"Daddy." It's a guttural groan. My voice isn't my own. I am fucking gone, so far gone that my eyes slam closed, my mouth rips away from his, and I'm tumbling like I've been caught in an undertow at sea. Only Griff isn't the riotous ocean. His hold is secure, he's my own personal life raft, and he doesn't seem to want to ever let me go.

8

GRIFFIN

Hook, line, and sinker. I've met the one woman who can match me move for move. Stormy's body is worn out from her orgasm, body lying against mine as I hold her tightly. No fucking way am I letting her go, not even for a night. I should have known the way she tossed back tequila, let go of her inhibitions, and had no problem tracking me down that she'd be it. I'm fucking gone for her in the best possible way. Add in the fact she's tight, so goddamn tight, it's a wonder Zach or any man before him couldn't make her come. Yet I did. Yet I fucking did, and she squirted, too. Her thighs are soaked, so are my hand and forearm, and I'm pretty sure my jeans. Not to mention the desk beneath her bare ass. I'm never going to want to clean it up either. I'll want the impression of her ass cheeks seared to the wood.

My brain quiets down. There's no bar, no Barbie, no worries about what my family, especially my brother, is going to think. In this moment, the only thoughts that consume me are Stormy and how I'm going to get us the fuck out of this place without people seeing her look as beautiful as she is right now.

"Hmm, I don't ever want to move." Her face is planted in my chest, her lips kissing right where my heart is currently beating rapidly. I don't want her to leave, and she clearly doesn't either, so it comes as no surprise when my hand burrows into her hair, holding her there.

"No one says you have to, baby girl." I kiss the top of her head, knowing we'll need to have a discussion. There are things we need to iron out and we'll need to make clear with one another.

"That's good because I'm not sure I can feel my lower extremities." There's a teasing to her tone. I look down at her with her skirt hiked around her stomach, her body suit contraption thing more or less a thong in the front and the back. I should have been more careful. Her legs are hanging freely off the edge of the desk. I'll bet she's got some tingling going on.

"Arms around my shoulders." I wait until she does as I request before picking her up and off the desk. Her legs wrap around me immediately. It does nothing for my cock, who refuses to go soft. A damn near impossibility when it comes to the woman in my arms. I walk with her until we make it to the couch in my office. Many nights, I found myself getting a few hours of shuteye before making the trek home. Especially in the early days, coming off a shift, landing at the bar, working from noon until three o'clock in the morning. I was dead on my feet and didn't need to be behind a wheel endangering myself or someone else. The couch has been a staple ever since, though now it's newer, not the hand-me-down I once had, and it's also deep enough that it's more than comfortable to use on a rare occasion these days.

"You good?" I ask once I settle us on the couch, her knees at either side of my waist, her arms still holding on, and the only difference? She's lifted her head, and I've got her pretty face looking up at me like I'm the keeper of her stars.

"Um, yeah, I mean, still kind of shocked.

That was pretty intense. Are you okay?" She drops down, her cunt pressing on my cock. Her squirming causes me to hold her hips so she can't do any more damage. As it is, I'm going to have blue balls with a permanent zipper etched into my dick.

"Ignore my dick. He can wait. We've got a few things to talk about before I'm taking you home." I can feel the change in her when I utter those two sentences. When she tries to back away from me, I keep her firmly in my hold. "Baby girl, if you think I'm taking you to your place, you're dead fucking wrong. You'll be in my bed tonight. What we do will be up to you." She settles down, no longer trying to get away from me.

"Okay." She doesn't argue the idea, so I figure it's time to get this conversation taken care of so I can do something about my never-ending hard cock, whether that means a cold shower, using my hand, or getting Stormy horizontal, spread out on my bed, and sinking so deep inside her we have a repeat performance of earlier.

"You like what we did?" I ask.

"Ugh, yeah, more than like. Didn't you get the memo?" She follows up a question with a question. I smirk, glad she's pleased with getting off as hard she did.

"I got it, baby girl, loud and clear. I know you like for me to be in control, I know what you sound like when you come and what you feel like doing the same. I also know you went off even higher when you called me daddy." Her cheeks pinken, her chest rises and then falls.

"About that. I've never, you know..." She fumbles with her words. That's okay because I've got all the patience in the world when it comes to Stormy talking. It doesn't matter if it takes her all night. I'll sit right here, holding her close, till it's all out. "Well, you know that I've never orgasmed with a man before. My drunken words were definitely sober thoughts. As for using the word *daddy*, that's a new level of myself unlocked, and yeah, I like it. A lot."

"Good, I like that I'm the first man you've experienced both with. I'm going to give it to you straight. This isn't me trying to take over your life or fulfill that role as a father. It's yours, and it's mine, no one else's." I let me words sink in, knowing she'll have questions. I'm ready and waiting to answer anything she's got, to navigate the newness that is taking hold between us.

"This, will it stay in the bedroom? Not that I'm against others having a full-time daddy thing. I just don't want to lose a piece of myself." The quiet time Stormy had coming down definitely gave her time to contemplate things. I shouldn't be surprised, yet I am. She's a strong, independent woman, got wrapped up in the wrong man thinking she was doing what most people her age need to do because society is a pain in the dick and dictates our way of thinking.

"No, baby girl, this gig is only in the bedroom. I'm not trying to staunch your personality. You're still you, and I'm still me." She breathes a sigh of relief. Her hands move from around my neck they are on my chest, kneading me like a kitten.

"I'd like that, a chance to navigate something new. And Griff?" she questions.

"Yeah, Stormy?"

"I should probably clean up. I'm kind of making a mess out of more than myself now." I don't give a Goddamn, but if we're going to walk out of the bar with an audience, I can understand her worry.

"Bathroom is through that door. I've got a spare shirt you can wear, then we'll head back to my place, yeah?"

"Okay, but no tequila this time. My liver is on a vacation from alcohol of any kind for the time being." She laughs. I chuckle. I bet her body is revolting at the thought of drinking since last weekend.

"Go clean up, so I can dirty you up again." I wrap my hand around the back of her neck to pull her closer, my lips a breath away from hers. "The next time you come, it'll be with my mouth and then my cock." Baby girl licks her lips, and there's no way I'm going to deny either of us the pleasure of a kiss. So, I do what I want when it comes to Stormy—I fucking take. I fuse our lips together, tongue snaking inside, unable to resist the urge to have another taste to hold me over until we're back at my place, where work isn't going to interrupt. There will be nothing but me and her, all night long.

9

STORMY

I walk into the bathroom trying to hide in the biggest, goofiest smile ever. It's hard to contain, and the only reason I'm able to do so is because I'm literally still flying high on actually coming. *Dear God, please don't let this be a fluke*, I pray to the orgasm gods. It seems lately, I'm always praying to one thing or another. What I'm not expecting when I flip the light on is how mussed my hair is, how plump my lips are, and how I've got a massive beard burn along my neck and chest. Not to mention my body suit is absolutely toast. Hopefully, Griff makes good on his promise and brings me a shirt. I don't think I'll be able to walk out of the bar with how stretched out the neck is. A shiver runs up my spine as I

replay writhing in pleasure with each movement Griff used to work my body into a fevered
pace. I take care of business, clean myself up
after using the bathroom, leaving the button
unsnapped. I wash my hands, splash water on
my face, and start the process of taking the
body suit off. No easy task with the light sheen
of sweat that's clinging to my body.

"Stormy, you good?" Griff knocks once,
turns the handle, and opens the door as my
head finally clears the bodysuit. I can only
imagine what I look like right now, plus the
fact I've got zilch on in the panties department.
Neither one of us are going to be able to wait
till we get to his place.

"Yep, I think this is going in the trash," I tell
him as I ball the fabric to toss it into the can
next to the toilet. His office has every modern-
day amenity. There's even a shower in the bathroom. Which might I add is awfully tempting.

"The fuck it is." Griff rips the suit out of my
hands and tosses it over his shoulder, leaving it
hanging there as he prowls toward me. The bar
shirt in his hand he went to find me is thrown
on the counter behind me. I'm left with no
other choice than to take another step back
until I'm met with the counter. His hands go
around my waist, thumbs sliding beneath the

lace cups of my bra. "I'm keeping this, forever. It'll stay in my desk drawer, and every time I open it, I'll get the scent of you, remember the thrill I was the one who gave you that, and maybe it'll tide me over until I have you again." Yet again, I'm left weak in the knees, this time from pressing my thighs together. It seems I'm always trying to relieve an ache that Griff creates. At least now I know he can take care of me, in more ways than one.

"Griff." My voice quivers.

"Say it, baby girl, say what you really want to say." His head descends, nose gliding along mine, and his thumbs graze the undersides of my breasts.

"Daddy." Giving over control to Griff is as easy as breathing. All I want is him in this moment, nothing else. His body dips, and he drags his length along me once again, eyes lazily watching how he's moving my skirt up again. This time, I'm baring it all to him; there isn't anything beneath, not even a small landing strip. I'm currently revolting against anything the name who shall not be spoken in my past told me made a woman look childlike. Too bad for him, he no longer controls me, and I find shaving it all smooth easier than maintaining a landing strip or dealing with shaving only my bikini area. It's been pure bliss taking it all off while shaving my legs, and I'm never going back.

"Fucking hell. I should wait. Damn it all to hell, I should have my first taste of you when it's not in a damn bar." He isn't talking to me; he's talking to himself, and honestly, I don't like what he's saying. Who cares where we are? All either of us should care about is what we want.

"Please," I moan when his nostrils flare. He takes a deep breath, and it's then I know he can smell me in the small bathroom.

"Not yet. We both wait, or we'll never leave." Clearly, he's holding firm. Not that I can blame him; it's been a long night, and he's yet to have any relief.

"Can I at least help you?" I ask, worrying that all I'm doing is taking and giving nothing in return.

"No." It's said with vehemence, almost taking me aback. "Not yet. I've got no damn control where you're concerned, baby girl, and you're not taking me in your hand or your mouth the first time."

"Oh, okay," I reply after he softens his tone. Griff is fierce in his words at times, and given we've just started to learn each other, it can be quite the curve to navigate.

"I promise when the time comes for you to take me into your hot mouth, I'll let you know. I'll also show you how I like it, baby girl." He rubs his jean-covered cock along my slit, eliciting a purr from me. My eyes close, and I'm lost in euphoria once again. "Fuck, I can't wait to see your cunt choke on my cock." He pulls away as the sound of his walkie talkie goes off.

"Griff, this is Nav, copy, you there?" Griff cusses under his breath. My hand is engulfed in his. I think to grab the shirt he tossed on the counter. I really hope he's not going to have me go out to the bar with my lack of underwear. That doesn't sound like a great idea to me.

"Nav, this is Griff, copy." His voice is tight, body locked up, and I can see his muscles punching beneath his shirt. I really miss seeing his unclothed chest and back. A girl could mourn the fact he hid it beneath cotton fabric.

"We could use some assistance out here. Got four live ones," Nav says over the speaker.

"Shit. Goddamn it all to fucking hell. These rowdy little dumb shits," Griff says out in the open before hitting the button and saying, "Copy, on my way." Then he's hooking it to his belt all while looking at me the entire time.

"Stay here, lock the door behind me, and don't open it for anyone but me." This is a different side of Griff, the bar owner side, which means he'll take no shit. Truth be told, I'm more worried about the men fighting than him.

"Okay." His lips meet mine for a light kiss, and then he's once again dragging me behind him until we're at the door.

"Lock the door. Food is in the fridge, so are drinks. I'm not sure how long this will take or if the cops will be called. As soon as I get this taken care of, we're leaving." I nod. "Fuck, I need one more taste." He dips his head, and his tongue slides along the seam of my lips, sucking my upper lip into his mouth and leaving me breathless all over again.

"Go, I'll be fine. Be careful, Griff," I tell him when he gives me his back, looking over his shoulder.

"Lock the door. Don't let anyone in." He's adamant about that, which is why I smart off.

"Yes, sir, Daddy." He shakes his head but walks through the door, shutting it behind him, and I click the lock into place. "Great, now I'm left in his personal space, and all I want to do is snoop." I'm not going to, though. I'm going to grab a bite to eat, a drink, settle in the couch, and maybe watch television to keep me occupied.

10

GRIFFIN

People always say to watch for the big guys, they'll hit you harder. They have no idea what they're fucking talking about. It's always the tall, leaner ones. The energy is like they've got enough damn drugs in their system to go round after round, not feeling a lick of pain. It took Nav, Jeremy, and me to subdue the four knuckleheads. There was no containing it away from the cops either. Another customer called, and while I'd have rather thrown their drunk asses out or in a hired car, really, nothing could be done.

"You good?" I ask Nav and Jeremy. The lights to the bar are on, and we're closing down early. There's no need to try and salvage another hour after the shit we all just went through.

"Yeah, man," Nav replies with a shiner developing around his eye. "Chicks dig banged-up guys." I look around the bar, not seeing a chick hanging around. Maybe he's off to another bar since we're closed.

"Get your shit done and go find one who will look at your ugly mug," Jeremy responds.

"If you have the cash registers closed down, I'll put the deposit in the office, and then I'm out for the night." Nav gets back to off-loading the coolers, pulling the drain plugs, and re-stocking the unused beer for Monday.

"They're done. The waitresses have already cashed out, too." I follow Jeremy to the main cash register he runs on the nights Barbie doesn't work here. Those two are the ones I can leave with the bar and know it's not going to catch on fire only to burn to the ground.

"Thanks," I say. Jeremy hands me the money bag.

"No problem. I'll lock up, make sure the trash is taken out, and then see you next week."

"It'll be Barbie and you next week. I've got a boat race to be at, so I'll be gone Thursday until Sunday," I tell him the same thing I did Barbie.

Usually, the two of them will talk, figure out who wants what days and nights, and then go from there.

"Alright, I'll text her tomorrow, and we'll let you know the days we choose," Jeremy states.

"Sounds like a plan. I'm out of here." I nod, rap my knuckles on the counter, and then make my way back to Stormy. I've been gone a lot longer than I thought I would. A brawl will do that. The paperwork and the four guys being taken to the drunk tank tonight made it impossible to be fast. I take a look around the dance floor along the way, noticing that it'll need to be waxed in the next couple of weeks. Another thing to add to my list once I return from the boat race. Making a quick mental note, I walk down the hallway leading me to my office, where Stormy should be on the other side. I told her not to open the door for anyone except me, and I'm sure she didn't. The key code would make it impossible, except for Barbie, who isn't here, and Jeremy, who knows Stormy's in my office, so he wouldn't even bother. My main concern was someone clumsy enough to make their way back here, up the stairs, and to bang on the only door, which is my office. It was enough to make me worry.

"Stormy." I knock on the door before putting the code in so she knows it's me coming in. I don't get a response as I twist the knob, open the door, and come to a stop.

"And she sleeps." My baby girl likes to burrow, it seems. There, in my shirt, arms tucked beneath her head and trying to melt into the back of the couch, Stormy sleeps peacefully. I close the door behind me, see that she ate the dinner I picked her up. The television is playing softly in the background, and I definitely need to add a blanket for her. My steps are quick to her. I place my hip to the cushion, my hand hovering above her cheek, wondering if waking her would be a good idea or if I should let her rest a bit longer.

"Stormy, baby, wake up for me." I make the decision she'll be more comfortable in my bed. No, *we'll* be more comfortable in my bed because while the couch and her sleeping on top of me is an appealing situation, there isn't a lot of room. The last thing I need is for her to roll over and land on the floor.

"Griff." Her eyes are still closed as she sinks into my hand that's cupping her cheek.

"Baby girl, I need you to wake up so we can head home." I'm wondering if she even realizes I'm here and touching her.

"Huh?" Her eyes open, and she blinks the sleep away. "What happened to your jaw? Oh my God, Griff, your lip is split." The once sleeping beauty is wide awake, sitting straight up and grabbing for my hand.

"I'm okay. Had to break up the fight, and it took longer than expected," I reply, seeing and hearing the worry in her face and her voice.

"Come on, I'm taking care of you this time." Fuck yeah, this woman. I'd let her do whatever the hell she wants, as long as it's not in the bedroom. I help Stormy up from the couch and let her guide me once we're standing and walk to the bathroom.

"The first aid kit is under the sink. Hop on the counter, and you can have your way with me." She flips the light on in the bathroom, and we both really see the damage. The cocksucker that took a swing at me did a stellar job to my jaw and mouth. It's a damn good thing none of my teeth are loose. Had that been the situation, I'd have really let him have it instead of only holding him down.

"Griff, for once, let someone help you out instead of helping everyone else. Sit on the toilet so I can clean you up. I'm pretty sure you don't need stitches, but a new shirt is in the works, too." Stormy's independent streak comes out. I oblige her, ready to get this over with, head to my place, and pass out with my baby girl in my arms.

"Fine. Did you eat enough?" I flip the seat down, doing as she asks as she opens the cabinet, grabs the first aid kit, and sets it on the counter. My eyes stay glued to her body as she washes her hands, then opens the kit to rip open a few antiseptic wipes before coming to stand between my spread thighs.

"I did, thank you. Though, I'm sure you didn't, and now eating is going to be hard for you," she says. "This is going to sting." My hands go to the back of her bare thighs. She wipes at the dried blood, then at the split above my lip. Meanwhile, I stay stone-cold still.

"I'll be fine. We'll take whatever is left to my place, and I'll finish it there." The tips of my fingers move up, and she presses the wipe deeper into my cut. This time, I'm unable to hold back a hiss. I guess that's what I get for having my way with her body while she works on me.

"All done, no stitches necessary. You're going to have a decent-sized bruise, though, and who knows how long it will take your lip to heal," she states, throwing away the used wipes.

She has no idea the only thing I'm pissed off about is the fact I'm not going to be able use my mouth on her pretty cunt until it is healed.

"Thank you." I stand up, reluctantly letting go of her thighs. "Let's go home." My cock is back to hard as a rock, and it's tired of being locked up behind my jeans.

"You're welcome." She puts the first aid kit away, washes her hands again, and I wait for her. "I'm ready whenever you are."

"Come on. I'll have Nav pull your car around the back. Then you can follow me to my place, unless you want to leave your car in the parking lot overnight?" I offer the last bit, but that doesn't mean I want her to actually do it. And not because it'll give the town of Jasmine more to talk about. I could give two fucks about what they think. It's not safe when I have a perfectly good two-car garage hers could be parked inside.

"I didn't drive," she replies.

"What do you mean you didn't drive. Did a friend drop you off?" I swear to Christ, if Stormy says she hired a car to bring her here, I'm going to spank her ass until she can't sit for a week.

"I walked. No offense, Griff, but parking

sucks here, and I didn't want to have to circle the block for hours until a spot opened up."

"You walked at night, during tourist season, from your place to here?" I question, making sure I heard her right.

"It only took ten minutes, and I had my phone out and ready to use if needed." It's far worse, far fucking worse. Jesus, the shit that could have happened to her, and she thinks a damn phone could have prevented something from happening.

"Stormy, no more walking. I'll come pick you up, or you can park at my house, and I'll pick you up from there if you're worried about parking. The last thing I want is for you to get hurt. At all." I bite back my anger, reluctantly.

"Fine. I still think it's a bit overreactive of you to think someone in this small town, tourists included, would do anything to hurt me." Maybe she's right, maybe she's wrong. I'd rather not take a fucking chance either way.

"Thank you. Now, are you ready to go?" She nods and skirts around me, hitting the fridge to pull out to-go bag that has the food in it. I watch as she picks up a few things that are scattered throughout my office. A hair tie on my desk, the pillow she knocked off the couch, and then she slides on her shoes. It's only when she's waiting at the door that I get the message she's ready to roll. That's when I walk toward her, take the bag out of her hand, open the door, and escort her out before turning around to make sure the door is locked behind us.

11

STORMY

"Fuck, I forgot to ask if you were okay with dogs?" Griff asks as he parks his truck in the garage of his beach house. I'm too busy trying to pick my jaw up off the floor. I knew Griffin did good for himself, and while his house isn't huge or of the newer builds, it's still pretty impressive, an older home, built in the seventies. Although it does look like it's been updated throughout the years.

"Stormy, did you hear me?" Griff asks, shaking me out of my stupor.

"Oh, sorry, what did you say?" My fingers are touching my mouth to make sure if I was drooling, I can at least wipe it away before he notices.

"Dogs, are you okay with them?"

"You have a dog? What kind of dog? What's his or her name? Tell me everything. And yes, I'm more than okay with dogs. I always wanted one when I was a little girl. Mom told me it wasn't feasible, single mom, working two jobs, me in school and sports. It never happened. Then as an adult, it didn't either. My job isn't exactly a nine to five, and my apartment doesn't allow pets of the four-legged kind." I go into far too much detail explaining that I'm good with dogs given the chuckle Griff lets out.

"I have a dog. Finn is a Golden Retriever and a total goof, lies around the house like the couch potato he is." The whole drive to his place, my hand was in his sitting on the center console of his truck. Even now, we're parked in his garage, and Griff has not let my hand go. It's like he's worried I'll sneak off on him. As if. The man is freaking amazing, and I've barely scratched the surface to everything Griffin Romero.

"Well, say less, lead the way." His hand leaves mine to turn the engine off, and I'm starting to go after the handle of the door, a second wind hitting me at the thought of hanging out with his dog.

"Don't even think about it, Stormy. Not sure

what the dumb fuckboy did for you. I'm gonna lay it out for you now. I'll open and close the door for you, probably smack your ass as you walk by while doing so. I'm a man's man, not this bullshit he's given you, or anyone else for that matter. I'm also going to make sure you're fed and that you come harder than you ever have." His voice started out gruff then got huskier toward the end. My thighs are never going to recover from the workout they're getting from being constantly clenched. "You hear me, baby girl?" And when Griff uses that name, it does nothing but set my body on fire.

"I hear you, Daddy." Using it outside of our sexual escapades doesn't feel weird. In this instance, I think it's pretty clear Griff is inserting his dominance, and I'm completely here for it.

"Fuck, you keep surprising me. Sit tight. I'll get your door, then I'll introduce you to Finn." I don't get a response mainly because he's already opening his door and hopping out of the truck. Which Griff makes look all too easy. Meanwhile, it's anything but easy for me. My eyes track his movements as he walks around the front of the truck. He never did change his shirt, saying he'd be taking it off when we got home and would be taking a shower. Damn, maybe I should have packed a bag. Clearly, this whole spending the night thing came out of the blue. I could have at least brought a purse, a change of panties, toothbrush, and a hairbrush. One look at the mirror earlier told me there was no taming my wild locks. As it is, I've got my phone that has a case to hold a card, my driver's license, and cash.

"Ready?" Griff opens the door, holding his hand out for me to take, probably to help me down, and if I weren't in a skirt, I'd probably slide down, then we'd start the whole him growling, me whimpering, and we'd never make it inside.

"Yep." I grab the bag of food I placed between my feet so it wouldn't tip over. My other hand goes to his, and he's helping me out of the truck. It's not even that high up. I'm just a slightly shorter size compared to Griff and half of the population of Jasmine.

"Ignore Finn when we get inside. His manners get away from him when he's excited, plus we don't get a lot of visitors at the house." Just because Griff is Melanie's uncle doesn't mean we all hung out together. He's older, she's young, well, I am too, and the circle of friend I surrounded myself with, it's obvious they're shit.

"I'm sure he'll be fine." He guides me to the door with a hand on my hip, the other out to turn the knob. I can hear the clicking of Finn's heels on the other side. "He must be excited. Who takes care of him when you work late at the bar or out of town?" I ask, wondering the logistics about how things work.

"I've got a neighbor who comes and lets him out. The only problem is Finn needs more exercise, so when I'm gone, he can get destructive if I leave something out and he's in a particular mood." Griff stands behind me as he opens the door. A ball of fur, yips, and excitement bolts toward us. "Finn, easy, boy." The Golden Retriever doesn't listen. He's too busy nudging my hand, and I'm too much of a softy to let him not receive my attention.

"Hi, Finn." I lift my hand out. Finn goes crazy, his big body wiggling, and then he's nuzzling into me. I get the go-ahead from him and Griff to pet him. Instantly, I'm in heaven.

"Easy, Finn," Griff states as Finn gets even more excited. How that's possible, I have no idea. "Come on, baby girl, let's go inside." He squeezes my hip. Finn is ignoring his owner and showering me with all the attention in the way of licking my hand.

"Why don't I take him outside to do his

business? You eat your cold dinner, and I'll join you after?" I offer, realizing yet again he hasn't eaten, and it's close to two o'clock in the morning. I'm exhausted, not hungry like I'm sure he is, and I'm pretty certain Griff must be tired, too.

"You taking care of me now, baby girl?" His lips graze me behind my ear. A shiver slides down my spine. I'm not sure if I'm taking care of him or being a decent human being, but if Griff likes the idea, I wouldn't be opposed either.

"Maybe I am. Does he go out through that door?" I point to the sliding glass door.

"He does. You sure you're okay with taking him out? He may keep you out longer than you expect." I'm pretty sure taking a dog outside won't take too much out of me and I'll be fine.

"Positive. Eat your dinner so we can go to bed." Finn must have to go because he starts running back and forth between us and the door.

"Thanks, baby. I'll walk you out there, then eat real quick." He guides me through the living room. I'm barely able to take it all in. The only light he has on is a lamp on the side table, and with the way Finn is moving, I'll have to take a look on my way.

"Go eat. I'm sure I won't get lost in the twenty or so feet I'll be away from you." This man, he doesn't turn off for a minute. Not even when he needs to take care of himself.

"I will. I'm just making sure everything is good in the backyard. We can't have a lot of lights on while it's nesting season for the turtles." When he puts it like that, it's kind of hard to say much else.

"Oh, well, okay." He unlocks the back door. Finn takes off, not a care in the world. Meanwhile, I stand on the concrete, face turned up toward the moon, enjoying the sounds of the waves crashing against the shore.

"Everything's good. I'll leave the door open. Come in whenever." I feel his finger graze along the outside of my arm. My flesh pebbles in his wake, making me want more of his tantalizing touch.

"Alright." My voice is breathless, and I realize just how stupid I was to stay with Zach. Especially when there's a man like Griff who is willing to put in the effort and work to make me believe there's something real out there and maybe I finally found it.

12

GRIFFIN

"Shower," I tell Stormy when she finally reappears with Finn at her heels. True to my words, my boy kept her out there for as long as he could. I grabbed my sandwich, walked back to the glass doors, and watched. Stormy never tired from throwing the ball back and forth with Finn. It was my boy who finally gave her mercy.

"Yes, please." A yawn escapes as she tries to cover it up with her hand.

"Come on, you're dead on your feet. I'm tired, and morning is going to come faster than either of us want. Finn doesn't care if he goes to sleep at nine at night or two in the morning. He's up like clockwork for his breakfast at eight o'clock." I lock the back door. My hand moves to her lower back, and I guide her through the house. My place is a one-story, three-bedroom, two-bath older style home with a few upgrades I've managed to do with my hectic schedule. I got lucky, managing to get grandfathered in with this location. A moratorium was put in place shortly after I purchased my home, stating nothing more than a two-story could be built in our neighborhood. Which means no fucking high-rise condominiums and no damn hotels.

"Well, I can't say I'll wake up with him after only a few hours of sleep." Can't say that I blame her. Finn also isn't her responsibility. I'll get up with him, let him out, feed him, and then slide back in bed. This time with Stormy wrapped around me.

"Not worried about that at all." I flip the switch to my bedroom light, and the wall lamps illuminate the room, each situated on either side of the king-size bed. The bed isn't made, which is the norm for me, but today I kind of wish I had the forethought to at least pick up a bit. The walls are beige, much like the rest of the house. Having it all one color was not only cheaper, it was also easier when painting. My bedroom set was handed down to me from my grandparents. Jack got other shit that I didn't see a need for. I got the better end of the stick, especially in the form of real wood furniture, while he got a collectable beer stein set. The fucking irony, I own a bar and would rather have the furniture. Meanwhile, Jack is a businessman through and through.

"Wow, this is beautiful." Stormy drifts away, running her fingers along the dresser. A dresser that took me far too long to sand and refinish.

"Thanks. Let me grab you a shirt, and I'll show you the bathroom." She moves away from the dresser, meandering around the room, landing at another set of sliding glass doors that lead out to the backyard. I make a mental note to close the blackout curtains. Maybe tomorrow, Finn will pull a solid and let me sleep in an hour or so longer than his usual. I move to where she was standing, pull open a drawer, and grab one of my well-worn shirts for Stormy.

"Stormy," I try to get her attention. She's lost in a daze, watching the moon illuminate the ocean. Sometimes I forget how lucky I am to have this as my backyard.

"Oh, sorry, what did you say?" This woman is forever in her own head, it seems, unless my hands are on her body.

"You ready for that shower?" She walks toward me in a slow gait, and damn it all to hell, I'm going to curse myself up and fucking down for what I'm about to say.

"Yes. You don't happen to have a spare toothbrush, do you?"

"Yeah, I got a spare. Not that I would mind you using mine," I reply. She follows me to one of the two doors in the same wall. The one to the left is the walk-in closet; the one on the right leads to the bathroom. I open the door, hopeful that it's not too much of a mess, and flip on another switch until the fan and light combo comes on together.

"Uhh, that's nice of you and all, to offer to use your toothbrush, but I'll take the spare." Her nose wrinkles.

"Baby girl, I've had my fingers on you, you've soaked me and my clothes. My mouth is going to be on you, and my dick is going to be inside you soon. Sharing a toothbrush isn't a bad thing." Towels are hanging up, toilet seat is down, and it's cleaner than I thought it would be.

"Well, when you put it like that..." She doesn't finish her thought. My hand wraps in her hair, tipping her head back. My head descends, lips sliding along the corner of her mouth.

"Take a shower. I'll meet you in the bedroom when you're done." I nip at her lower lip, licking it when I'm done to soothe away the bite.

"You're not showering with me?" There's disappointment in her tone, and damn if the invite isn't tempting.

"Not this time. I get in the shower with you, and we're not going to make it to bed for hours. We're both tired, and while I want nothing more than to slide into my baby girl's body, we both need rest. Tomorrow, I'll take you in the shower, in my bed, on the damn kitchen counter, and I promise you it'll be worth the wait." Stormy's body sways toward me, melts against me, and damn if this isn't harder than I thought it would be. My cock is mourning the loss even though it's never even been inside her.

"Oh, okay." Her eyes shutter, and she's looking downward and no longer at me. Fuck, the last thing I want is for her to think I don't want her or for her to revert inside herself and think this is a Zach situation.

"Stormy, I'm not half-assing this. Take your sweet-as-fuck ass in the shower. I'll meet you in my bed. It means something to me. It means everything to me, especially given what you've told me about your past. So, take that sweet ass in the shower. I'll use the one down the hall. Get in my bed and wait for me." I hand her a shirt again. The woman is going to have half my wardrobe soon.

"Well, when you put it like that, it makes more sense. Do you have a pair of shorts or boxers to go along with this?" She holds up the gray shirt.

"When you're in my bed with me in it, no panties, no shorts. I don't want anything hindering me from having you." I dip my hips, letting her feel what the thought of having her in my bed with nothing but my shirt on does to me.

"Yes, Daddy." My name comes out as a sigh.

"Good girl. Be back soon." I leave before I take back what I said and join her in the shower. I'm already going to have to take care of my hard cock. Hopefully, this will be the last time. I've been walking around with blue balls and a permanent zipper impression. Jesus, I'm tired of my own fist fucking my cock. A few more hours. I can hold out until then. The only question is, can Stormy?

13

GRIFFFIN

When I got into bed last night, Stormy was already passed out. She must have taken a faster shower than I did. Probably because I rubbed one out, my cum splashing against the tile and the water washing it down the drain. When I slid in beside her, she turned toward me, hand going to my stomach, head on my chest, and I got a soft sigh from her. I settled in, found sleep and comfort with the woman wrapped around me. Finn woke up entirely too early, like I knew he would. He went outside, took care of business, came back inside for food, and then promptly fell back asleep on the couch. Where I know I'll find him again later, his back to the couch, paws up, and snoring.

Now I'm wide awake. Stormy is still asleep, and I'm ready to make good on my promise. I'm lying behind her, my arm beneath her neck, the other pulling up her shirt to reach more of her soft skin.

"Hmm," she moans. My fingers inch their way up the middle of her stomach, hand finally reaching her breast. I cup it, fingers plucking at her nipple. Her ass arches back into my groin. It's a damn good thing I had the forethought to lose my shorts. Last night, she was dead to the world asleep. I don't think anything could have woken her up, and I certainly wasn't going to be like 'Hey, do you mind if I sleep naked?' No damn way, not when she's bare beneath my borrowed shirt.

"Baby girl, time to make good on my promise on making you come, repeatedly," I murmur into her ear, feeling the shiver that runs through her body. My hand that was working her nipple travels down her stomach, taking in each slope and contour until I make it to her drenched pussy. Even in her sleep, Stormy is ready for me. Goddamn, I'm a lucky fucking man. She feels damn good, body undulating into my fingers.

"Daddy." Son of a bitch. My cock hardens.

I'm not sure how that's possible, but with Stormy, it seems anything is likely to occur.

"Going to give you my dick, baby girl. Are you gonna be a good girl and take it?" I ask, pulling my hand away from her cunt. She groans in annoyance. Stormy has my cock throbbing against my abdomen, and though she lost my hand on her slit, it won't mean I'm leaving her for long.

"Yes," she purrs through a sleep-induced fog.

"Yes, what?" My cock slides along the lips of her pussy, coating the top half with wetness. Fuck, I'm ready to say screw the teasing and slam my length inside her.

"Yes." Her voice hitches when my tip hits her clit. "Yes, Daddy," Stormy replies when I drag my hips back, repeating the leisurely process.

"That's right, baby girl. I'm going to give you my dick. You're not going to move. I want you to stay still, hands wrapped around my neck, and don't fucking let go." I pull my hips back, keeping her leg hiked over my hip. She is open and more than ready, even though I know for a fact it's going to be a tight fit. Which is why I'm trying to take my time. Hurting her is the last thing I want to do. Even if it's for our mutual benefit at the time, there's also no way one time with her is going to be enough. That means going slow is the only option for now. I notch the head of my dick at her entrance, feeling her lips flare around me, slick and ready. I push in an inch. Fucking fuck, she's like a damn vice, and I'm not even halfway inside. Yeah, the other needle nose dicks she's had in her past are nothing compared to the size of me, probably part of the reason she's yet to come with a man.

"More, please more." She is keeping her body still. Her fingers, on the other hand, well, that's an entirely different story. They're flexing and pulling on my lower neck, and I'm not seeing one single problem with that.

"Nice and slow," I counter, pulling my hips back until my cock isn't inside her sweet wet heat anymore.

"No, hard and fast." Yeah, fucking right, over my dead body. She's not prepared for that yet.

"Yes." I slide forward, my cock going in a bit further this time, and it must be enough to make her happy. Her breathing hitches, words dying in the back of her throat, and my dick is being sucked into her cunt.

"Jesus, baby girl. Your pussy is trying to

suck me dry." If I hadn't jerked off last night, there's no way I'd be able to last as long as I want to. And what does that say about me, besides the fact it's been too damn long?

"Oh God, it feels so good. Don't stop this time, please," she begs. I'm not sure I could even if I tried. Leaving her cunt is like asking me to leave her. It'll never fucking happen.

"You better tell me if it gets too much," I grunt, pushing my hips forward. My hand that was beneath her neck is now on her tit, my palm full. The other is inching its way toward her center.

"It's not enough." Damn feisty woman.

"Stay still, or you'll lose my dick completely." She arches back, trying to wiggle her way down my length. My palm flattens on her lower abdomen, stopping her from moving again. The last thing she needs to do is slam her tight little snatch down my dick. Stormy is damn near virgin tight with every inch I feed her.

"No, don't do that. I'll stay still, promise." Her head tips over her shoulder, eyes going to mine, and fuck if that doesn't do something inside me. It settles deep in my chest, knowing she's locked on me and only me.

"Mouth, now," I groan when I'm halfway

inside. My middle finger slides to her clit, working her up until she's in a fevered pace before I add more pressure. I take her lips with mine, slow and soft at first while my cock continues the same torturous pace for both of us. I'm at my breaking point, her back to my front, our skin slick with perspiration. Her breathing is labored, and damn if it doesn't do something to me.

"Daddy." Fuck me sideways, taking this slow when my name leaves her, low, with that rasp in her tone, is testing my control. My tongue slides along the seam of her lips until she opens for me, allowing me to gain entrance. Our tongues tangle, me leading and Stormy following. I add another finger to the mix. Her wetness is more than enough to give her the sensation and friction she needs to stop clamping so hard on my cock I can finally be completely inside her. I move my fingers up and down, side to side. Her breath stutters. Her tongue doesn't slide along mine. In fact, she's pulled her head away from mine. A long deep, guttural moan comes deep from in, and I take that as my clue to pull my hips back and thrust all the way inside her.

"Fuck yeah, do you feel me? You have all of me." Her eyes close, and she takes a deep breath. Whether that's for her or me, I have no idea, but damn, my dick is loving exactly where it's at. I flex inside her, she trembles beneath my touch, and I take the time to continue working my hips back and forth. The slow easy glide is now gone. There's no way I can hold back, or I'll come before she does. And that's not fucking happening. She'll get hers before I'll get mine. There's no other way. She's being such a good girl, staying still while I use her body, working her in such a way she'll become addicted to me. Because there's no doubt about it, I'm addicted to Stormy. More than the next adrenaline rush, whether it's from a bar fight or jumping out of a helicopter to rescue a racer.

"Oh God." I flick her clit on another thrust. This time, there's no stopping the fast rhythm I've set, there's no slowing down. I'm chasing our orgasm. We will both come together, now and forever.

"Baby girl," I groan. Her ear is right by my mouth. My teeth nip at the lobe. Her cunt tightens its vice-like grip on my cock. Never thought it'd get tighter, but here we fucking are. The will to fucking live is hard when all I want to do is allow my body to take over. Finally, she starts to fall apart around me.

"Coming inside you, unless you tell me otherwise."

"Come inside me." Another thrust. She continues through each deep breath. "I'm protected." I hit a deep spot inside her, and Stormy barely has the wherewithal to finish yet does. "Had tests. We're good." Say fucking less. One more shove of my hips, her hands digging deeper into whatever she can find purchase on behind my neck, and Stormy lets go.

"Daddy." That fucking does it. My palm flattens on her cunt, fingers on either side of her clit, pinching it once, prolonging her orgasm as mine comes. I roll my hips and then let go. Jesus, never have I come this fucking hard. On each piston of my hips, another thick jet of cum leaves my body and coats the inside of her pussy. Son of a bitch, I'll never leave her now.

"Stormy," I groan her name as I finish. Being buried inside of her is now my home . Where she goes, I'll go. Day or night, rain or shine, I'm never letting her leave.

14

STORMY

"Oh shit." I roll over after falling back asleep after coming around the length of Griff's dick. That was round one. Round two consisted of him tunneling in and out of me with only the tip. Seriously, how was that even possible? I have no idea. All I know is I was a whimpering, quivering mess, and Griff pulled out of me at the last second and came all over my thighs and pussy.

"Go back to sleep, baby girl. It's still early." I'd love nothing more than to close my eyes and ignore the outside world. Sadly, I can't, or I'm really going to be homeless. Griff's arm is slung over my lower stomach, hand cupping my center, holding me to him during the entirety of our nap.

"I can't. I've got an appointment to look at an apartment." What was I thinking making an appointment on a Sunday? Oh yeah, that's right. Six more days.

"Reschedule it." He strums my clit with the pad of his finger, and if I weren't desperate to find a place, I'd forget all about this appointment.

"Griff, I would if I could." I moan when he hits the perfect spot, plunging two thick fingers inside me, the palm of his hand working my clit now. Jesus, he's a magician with the way he works my body.

"One more time. Give me one more, baby girl. Then we'll start our day." He's not playing fair, and I'm the one who's going to be left without a place to go.

"If I miss this appointment, I'm going to be living in boxes on the street corner." That has Griff moving us until I'm flat on my back, and he's wedging open my legs and settling between them.

"What do you mean, you'll be living in a box. What haven't you told me?" Damn, maybe I shouldn't have said anything, then I'd at least get one more orgasm before I have to admit my shortcomings. Though, the look on Griff's face says I'm not going anywhere until we have this out. Except his cock is happy to see me, and it has me hiking my legs around his waist trying to diffuse the situation before I dive back into reality. "Quit stalling, Stormy." I take a deep breath, careful not to blow it toward his face because morning breath. Even then, Griff comes down on both forearms, boxing me in, pulling my chin up to look into his eyes. I guess it's now or never, except the never won't be coming.

"You know my apartment lease is up. I tried to renew it, but it was already rented out. Every apartment I've looked at this week is either months out or so out of my price range I'd have to eat ramen noodles and peanut butter sandwiches in order to survive." I take a deep breath and keep going, "Add in the fact I'm not an hourly employee and live off of tip. It kind of makes it hard to show I have an influx of money, minus what's in my savings. Still, they don't care about that. They want you to make three times your monthly rent, and we're in the busy season of our small town, which makes it even harder."

"So, what you're saying is, you've got a lock on an apartment that's out of your price range, but you're willing to do whatever it takes." He looks at me like I have two heads. What else does he expect me to do? I mean yes, one day, I'd love to buy the salon from Kitty. But until she's ready and I've got more cash in my savings account, that day is not today. Sure I could put a down payment on a house, I'd rather not with how freaking topsy turvy my current situation is.

"Basically, it's that or live with my mom and aunt. There's live with them, in a cardboard box, or pay the price to have my own place." The last one won't happen. I'll move in with the two crazy sisters if need be. It's just my damn pride that makes me feel like I've got something to prove. And damn this town, too. Never before did I not love where I lived, but after Zach and Mel, it's all consuming. The walk to Griff's bar last night was done with my head down while still keeping a watchful eye out. Seriously, that was no easy task.

"Or you can move in here." I feel my eyes bulge, knowing my mouth is slack-jawed because who is this man?

"Are you feeling okay? Do you have a fever? Did the fight last night cause a concussion?" My hand cups his cheek, feeling his stubbled jaw. There's no fever. In fact, he's cool to the touch. The bruising on his jaw is developed and is turning that nasty shade of blue and purple. Griff's lip isn't much better, scabbing more, and it will definitely take a while to heal.

"Stormy, this place is big enough for the both of us. I'm not going to be home next weekend as it is. The neighbor does a decent job with Finn, but you see how he is. My boy needs love and attention. Clearly, he's infatuated already, and you'd be doing me a solid." He must think I'm going to agree right away. He dips his body, dragging his hard length along my wet slit.

"I'll watch Finn, stay and house sit, but moving in?" I leave the question open for interpretation.

"You think after last night, I'm going to let you go? Baby girl, we mesh, inside the bedroom as well as out. I'd be stupid not to lock this down. You think I give a flying fuck what this town has to say or that I don't know we're going to face a shit storm?" Okay, he does have some merit to his points, and also, the butterflies in my stomach are definitely happy that he's laying it all out.

"Why do I feel like I'm going to be persuaded if I say no?" My legs tighten around his thick waist. Griff rocks into my body. He's

working me into saying yes while I melt for
him. He knows it, and I know it. The only thing
left is for me to take a leap of faith. I should be
gun shy. My instincts have sucked thus far
when it comes to men. Zach did me so dirty,
Mel even more so, and she was my friend. The
difference is, Griff is not them, and he shows
me with every single thing he does. I dated
Zach for a year. He asked me to marry him on
the anniversary of said one year of dating. We
had a short engagement because his mom was
in Operation Marry Us Off as fast and as
expensive as possible. Maybe she knew something I didn't, though it's her smearing my
name in the dirt all over Jasmine. There's no
one else who would. The two other culprits are
currently on a vacation, thankfully.

"Because you'll say yes. If I have to fuck you
until you say it, I will." He's reminding me of
last night when he had to pull out in order to
ask me about birth control. I told him the
truth, that I was covered and also received my
test results back after finding out Zach was a
big fat cheater. Though, I'm thankful we had
yet to do away with condoms. I still wasn't
taking any chances.

"Fine, but I'm not unpacking all of my
crap." Griff blows out a puff of air, mutters

something under his breath, and tips his head toward the ceiling. "Not yet at least. We could get on each other's nerves. I mean, I'm not a huge slob, but I don't want this to end badly either."

"I'll give you that, but your clothes are in this room. You want to unpack or not, you can do it in your time, or we'll get you a storage unit. I've got a two-car garage, and I'd rather your car not be parked outside. Which means boxes can go in the spare room, but we'll have to figure out the other stuff." Okay, he's agreeing to this way too easily.

"I'm not bringing any furniture with me. I sold most of it. Mattress is on the floor, and the barstools aren't worth paying storage for. The same could be said about my couch and coffee table." Wow, it hits me all at once. I was willing to give everything away for a man who willingly threw me away like yesterday's trash.

"Good, that's settled. Now I'm going to make you come. We'll get started on moving you in today. That way, it's done before I leave on Sunday." I'm awarded with Griff's panty-melting smile, and lucky for me, I'm not wearing any.

15

STORMY

"So, do you think I'm making the right choice?" I ask my mom and aunt a day later. In my heart and gut, this feels natural, but that little girl inside of me is worried what the people I love the most will think. It's stupid, I know that to the depth of my being. My mom is not one to put conditions on love, and my aunt isn't either, for that fact.

"I think only you can answer that." We're at my apartment, cleaning it up so I can turn my keys in to management. While also picking up the last few stray boxes that Griff's truck and my car couldn't hold. His spare room is officially packed full of boxes, mostly books, decorations that I couldn't part with, and things I've collected along the way. I didn't even have much in the way of kitchen stuff because yet again, I'm an idiot. Zach and I would have had duplicates. He had the fancier stuff, whereas I had the clearance section items. So, it was smarter to come with less. Which is why I'm partially worried about the newest decision I've made. Is it smart to go from one man to the next so soon? It's obvious Griff is not at all like Zach, but man, I'm a freaking mess while over-thinking life lately. Another difference besides the orgasms I get from Griff versus none from Zach is that Griff didn't complain once about all my stuff. Whereas Zach had to make some smart-ass comment saying books can be donated, use an e-reader. Well, newsflash, psycho Zach, I use both. But nothing, and I mean nothing, beats opening up a book and holding it in your hands while you devour each word on the page.

"Stormy, what your mom is trying to say is this. Live your life to the fullest. You're going to experience heartbreak, embarrassment, and all kinds of things in between," Aunt Cat says.

"You can say that again, well, minus heart-break. When I found out Zach was with Mel all I felt was relief." God, that feels good to admit to others besides myself.

"You dodged a bullet," Mom interjects. We

laugh for a minute, and my nerves calm down that the two of them would think I was making a massive mistake.

"Back to the point at hand. If I were twenty years younger, honey, and a man like Griff was willing to give it his all, plus unlimited orgasms, I wouldn't be walking, I'd be running toward him." Aunt Cat's theatrics always crack me up. Even right now, she has a straight face, so I know she's not kidding, but with her yellow gloves, hair scarf, and all white clothes, it's kind of hard to ever take her seriously. I'm kind of shocked she didn't come wearing a hazmat suit given the fact cleanliness is most definitely next to Godliness in her eyes.

"Shut up, Cat. No one wants to hear about orgasms from you, or my daughter receiving them." Mom points her finger at her sister. "Let me ask you a question." She unpacks one of the boxes that needs to go to Griff's. I couldn't close the box, and I didn't want what is inside to get ruined.

"Mom, we're supposed to be moving out, not taking things out of boxes." My collection that isn't vintage romance books appears. I'm talking finds from a thrift store, Jane Austen and Emily Brontë to name a couple. Except I have many different volumes that I've found here and there.

"I'm well aware. I also know you've added something to this collection since what was supposed to be your wedding day." The brick she pulls out with different-colored feathers appears, and there, in the very front, is the newest one. I've been collecting them from the beach on certain occasions—my sixteenth birthday, graduating high school, becoming a hair stylist, certain memorable occasions. "So, tell me. Do you have one you found the day of your engagement? Because I know you, Stormy. You are your mother's child. We keep things that mean something to us. You've always been fond of feathers at the beach, bringing them home, washing them, and adding them to your collection. But only on a day that means some-thing to you." Jesus, my mom knows me a little too well.

I walk over to where she has the block with feathers standing up. None of the feathers I've taken are prohibited by the Migratory Bird Treaty Act. One day, I was about to pick a feather up when an older gentleman clued me in to the fact that some feathers are illegal to keep. From that point on, I studied each one or found what type of bird it came from with a quick search on my phone.

"So, when did you add this one to your collection?" Aunt Cat interrupts. I close my eyes. It would have been hard to keep it away from Griff when we were on the beach, and I was drinking as much as my body would allow me to. I wasn't upset about the lack of wedding; I was upset that I let myself go along with it when my instinct was telling me to run far away as fast as I could.

"The night Griff rescued me from a nightmare I allowed to be created." I open my eyes, feeling calmer.

"And there you have it. Heartache is hard, sweetheart. But missing out on love is worse," Mom says, putting her arms around me, hugging me. I also realize maybe my mom has been through a broken heart that was far worse than when my dad walked out on us without a backwards glance. The only thing I don't know is when or how it happened. My whole life growing up, Mom was adamant about not bringing men around when I was home. A few dates here and there when I was in high school was all I heard. In a small town, it's near impossible. Unless this is a recent development.

"Mom, you're allowed to find love, too, you

know." I blink back the tears, worried she's put her whole life on hold for me. I'm old enough now, twenty-four years old to be exact. Dad has been gone since I was eight. It's time for her to find her happily ever after.

"I know. Tell that to Aunt Cat. She's the one who can't find a man she likes. I'm learning it's time for me to start living again. It's hard when your identity has been a mom and a worka-holic for so long." I squeeze her tighter, more for myself than for her. She's given me abso-lutely everything a daughter could ask—any sport I wanted to try, and any time I needed extra help in a subject, she helped or found a tutor. Now the sham of a wedding she probably worked overtime to pay for, damn it. I'm going to make sure she's paid back, no matter what. Even if that means picking up new clients, working longer hours, or asking Griff if he needs help waitress a couple of nights a week.

"I love you, Mom, thank you." She has no idea what I'm grateful for at this point in time. One day soon, I'll make sure she knows.

"I love you, too." We pull back from out hug. "Okay, let's get this place cleaned up and get my girl out of here. I want to treat you to lunch. Next week, you'll be back at work, and these random days and spending time with you will come to an end."

"Oh, just you hush. I want in on the hug." Aunt Cat comes up behind me, grabs both of Mom's shoulders, and hugs us while smooshing me between the two of them. We all laugh, kind of like old times.

"I say it's time we get Aunt Cat out in the dating world. Know of any eligible bachelors?" Aunt Cat talks in third person.

"Dear God, the woman has more men after her than she can keep up with. Last week, one was pounding at the door because your aunt forgot it was date night!" Mom exclaims. Aunt Cat is like Blanche from Golden Girls. There's no man too old or too young for her. Plus, she's all about the free love and orgasm life. Yes, I'm aware I know entirely too much about my aunt, but she enjoys sharing with the class or the town. Whichever listens more. God love the man who finally ties her down.

"Aunt Cat! Did you forget your little pink calendar?" We break away from one another. I pick up my feather collection and put it back in the box. My fingers slide over the brown- and white-spotted feather, being careful. It really is one of the favorites in the group. It could be because of Griff or the uniqueness to it. Right now, I'm not completely sure, and that's okay.

"She did not. You know Cat doesn't leave that thing anywhere." Mom blows out a huff of air. Exaggerating the story is coming next.

"Well, actually, I didn't forget about him. He wasn't my type. My thought was maybe your mom would go out with the guy instead. That backfired when she went to her room, locked the door, and wouldn't come out." Aunt Cat acts like she's put out by this fact.

"I'm not going on a date with your second choice. And I'll have both of you know, I have a date tomorrow night." I squeal in excitement, happy for my mom.

"Oh my gosh, I'm so happy for you, Mom!" I'd offer to touch up her hair, but we just did that last week. That leaves her with finding an outfit, makeup, and to tame her beautiful waves in the summer humidity.

"The wheels are turning, aren't they? I can see it in your eyes. I'm good, Stormy. I've already got everything picked out, and if my hair doesn't cooperate, then fuck it." She's a damn mind reader. I nod anyways, wanting her to continue. Cleaning is going to be put to the side. Finally, my mom is doing something for herself, and I am freaking ecstatic.

16

GRIFFIN

"What's up?" I answer the phone seeing it's Jack's name on the display screen. The last thing I need is for my brother to give me shit when my head is focused on packing my bag for the weekend. I've already got the bar covered. Stormy is moved in, and we're settling in. Except for Finn, the fucking traitor, he only wants my woman. She also spoils him with walks twice a day, feeding him fruits and vegetables as snacks, and constantly has his head in her lap when mine isn't.

"You ready for this weekend?" He follows up my question. Figures he'd call to make sure I'm okay. Neither of us has broached the giant elephant in the room, and I'm hoping he doesn't do it right now. I've got more important shit to deal with than his daughter, my niece being a conniving cunt. In a way, I should be thankful. Never would I have gone after Stormy when she was with Zach, and before that she was way too young.

"As ready as I'll ever be." This boat race is three days long. Friday is a practice round, Saturday is qualifying, and Sunday is the finals.

"Listen, I'm putting it out there because you know this town talks. Mel and Zach will be back Sunday. She's already called and asked if we can have a family get-together." You gotta be fucking kidding me. I take my baseball cap off my head, run my fingers through my hair, and toss the cap on the bed. This is not what I want to deal with. Stormy is currently out on the beach with Finn, wearing a barely-there bikini, and I'm stuck in here for the time being. Luckily for me, I've got a clear view out to the beach. She's throwing the ball for Finn while I'm packing my suitcase.

"Alright, let me know a time and what day. I'll make sure Stormy's good with it, and we'll go from there." Jack's aware of what Mel and Zach are doing. Kind of hard not to in this town or when the bride-to-be and I didn't show up. Plus, she fessed up to her dad before they left. There's still a lot Jack doesn't know, and it's not my story to tell. Stormy keeps a lot close to her chest, not that I can blame her.

"Sounds good. You need me to stop by the bar or your house for Finn?" Jack asks this every time I'm out of town. He may be ten years older than me, and we practically grew up like only children, but we still look out for one another. He's been single for fifteen years. Mel's mom was caught on her knees with one of Jack's associates at the engineering firm he owns. Since she left, he's stayed a bachelor, and the only woman he has his eyes set on is Barbie, who refuses to give him the time of day. Which means I hear it from both sides.

"Barbie's got a handle on the bar. I figure you'll stop by anyways. You want me to text you the schedule, so you know when she's working?" I chuckle and abandon packing my bag. There's no way I'm going to get it done when I could be outside with Stormy.

"Yep, it'd make it easier than stopping by twice a day." Jack won't admit he wants Barbie, and Barbie won't admit she has her eye set on my brother. A bunch of fucking drama queens.

"Will do. As for Finn, Stormy's living here now, and you better not even think about fucking stopping by either." Finn trots back to my woman, proud as a damn peacock, ball in his mouth and wagging his tail. I'll just bet when I get back home, my dog won't so much as say hello to me and will more than likely take my place in our bed.

"It's like that, huh?" Jack says with a chuckle. This dickwad, he knows if roles were reversed, and this were me talking about Barbie, he'd lose his mind.

"It's exactly like that." I hit the speaker button, toss my phone on the bed, and take off my shirt. As soon as I'm off this call, I'm going to join my woman and traitor of an animal.

"Then I won't stop by, give her my number just in case something happens. That's if she can get past what Mel did and realizes it's not something I condone either. Fuck, my daughter is turning out to be her mother, Griff." We've yet to meet up and talk about this shit. It's hitting him hard, which I knew it would. Hell, it's pissed me off that my niece could do something like this to a friend she's known since high school.

"I'll do that. Stormy is pretty levelheaded. She's aware this is on Mel and Zach, nothing more or nothing less. As for Mel turning into her cunt of a mother, don't hold yourself accountable. Not once did you think it was okay to stick with a cheater or condone it. You've raised Melissa to go down a certain path. She veered off said path, and it has nothing to do with you." A heart-to-heart conversation isn't what I had planned for, but when your brother needs a minute, you give it to him.

"Yeah, you're right. I know you are. I just didn't expect it to lead to this. Mel has no idea what she's going to come back to once the truth comes out." Yeah, the whispers are running wild already. I'm sure it's Zach and his crew pinning this all on Stormy, especially with the way we left the ceremony—her dress in shambles, my hand on her bare back. Sure, I could have given her my suit jacket, but there was a sick part of me that wanted people to believe she was mine. I wasn't around much when Mel was in high school, not even through her college years either. Too busy chasing the dollar, so I had no idea of knowing much about Stormy until I came back a few years ago and started planting some roots. I'd see her here and there, wave hello, admire her beauty, but I kept my fucking hands to myself. She was already tied to douchebag Zach, way too young, or so I thought. And now, here we are. There's no damn way I'd ever let her go now.

"All you can do is love her, man. The rest is up to Mel. I appreciate you looking out for the bar and being a line of communication for Stormy. I'll touch base when I can." My swim trunks are already on. I'm ready to hang up and spend the remainder of my time with Stormy.

"The least I can do. Alright, go spend time with your woman, and be safe, brother." Jack gets the memo, thank fuck.

"Will do." We hang up. The half-packed duffel bag can wait. I grab my baseball cap. My sunglasses have been hijacked by a raven-haired beauty who's currently trying to kill me with the white bathing suit she's wearing. A tie at the back of her neck and between her fantastic fucking tits, following the ties on each side of her hips. I've got plans for how I'm going to undress her. I'll put on each bow with my teeth until Stormy is baring it all to me.

"God fucking damn it," I mutter under my breath, looking down at my cock. The struggle is real whenever she's around or whenever I'm thinking about her. Now I've got to figure out how to get my cock to go down. The damn thing's so hard it could cut glass.

17

STORMY

"Are you sure you'll be okay with Finn?" Griff has been asking me the same question in a variety of ways at least once a day this week.

"I'm positive. The big oaf and I have things to do. It's my last few days of being a lady of leisure," I joke. I'm cuddled into Griff's side on the couch, my head in the crook of his neck, and his fingers sliding up and down my arm in various patterns. Finn is sitting next to me, head on my lap in its usual place. I've got my hand on the inside of Griff's thigh, my other on Finn, scratching his ear while he edges even closer than I thought humanly possible.

"I can cancel. They've got enough guys on

this trip." That's news to me. He's worried. I'm not sure what about since I don't plan on doing a lot minus open my books for new clients. Which, let me tell you, is going to be a pain in the ass. The thought alone makes me want to re-think things. It's the booking an appointment and not showing up, the consultations where a box-dye brunette wants to become platinum blonde in one day, and then there are always the older ladies who come in asking for perms. I'll do all of them, especially the last, regardless of the smell, but I'll be grinning and bearing it the entire time. Sadly, it doesn't look like I'm going to have a choice if I'd like to keep a cushion in my bank account while figuring out what to do next.

"Why would you cancel? This has been on the books forever." Griff has a wall calendar in the kitchen with the dates he'll be out of town. It's at least one weekend a month for the next six months. I've looked and brought my book out with my clients and started working on rescheduling them when I could, going so far as to work on Sundays. That way, when Griff is out of town, I can work the whole weekend and save the rest of my Saturday mornings for him.

"Not really thrilled with the idea of leaving

you yet." Insert my inner girl squeal. Trying to control how happy his words make me is not going to be easy. The harder part is holding back throwing my body into his, climbing onto his lap, and watching his family jewels—well, they're even harder. Finn gets excited and jumps down off the couch, barks once, vying for our attention. Too bad, baby boy. There's a man who has it all—my eyes, my body, my heart, and my soul. It should say a lot about the fact that Griff has given me more in the couple of short weeks I've known him than Zach did in the years we were together. I should feel horrible about the feelings I've developed for Griff because they're so much more than I ever expected or experienced.

"I love that. Really, I do, and while a selfish part of me wants you to stay, the sensible part of me knows you're scheduled, and they would have called you off if they didn't need you." Griff's hands go to my hips, pulling me closer. I settle until my core is pressed against his further hardening cock. I awarded with a grin, the slightest bit of his perfectly straight and white teeth. I'll bet he didn't go through two sets of braces or headgear to get them either. Griff has it all. Don't get me wrong, I'm sure he worked for it. Especially his body. I've felt him leave me early in the morning, take Finn out, and it's not his usual fast morning production. Griff will be gone for an hour or so, then either slide into bed with me fresh from a shower, or on the rare occasion, he'll make it known that I'm needed in the shower with him. An occurrence that happened yesterday morning. I was snuggled in bed, my arms wrapped around Griff's pillow, sleeping peacefully. He had other plans, ripping the comforter off my body, and I was no longer warm and cozy. His hands wrapped around my ankles, and he literally pulled me away from my sleep. I moaned and groaned while simultaneously being turned on when he picked me up, my legs wrapping around his waist as he walked us to the bathroom. Shower sex is hot to experience. It's even hotter when your man is Griffin Hawkins. Though I never call him Griffin, and most others don't either

"I know I don't need to. I'm offering it just the same. You think it's entirely for you. It's not, baby girl. I'm greedy and selfish when it comes to being around you." His fingers knead my lower back. My eyes close, tears are trying to form in, and I'll be damned if I cry. Griff is leaving in less than an hour, and it's not like he's going away for months on end. It's just everything. He's a giver through and through. Giving me his words is enough to have me blinking away the years.

"Griff." He pulls me into his body, hands sliding up my back. My head settles into the crook of his neck, where I breathe in his scent deeply. I don't say anything else, and neither does he. We revel in the silence, the two of us along with Finn.

"Stormy, you start crying, and I'll make the call now to stay home." That pulls me out of my reverie. There's no way I'll allow him to not go.

"I'm good, promise. You've given me so much, and it hit me like a ton bricks. I've yet to bring as much to the table as you have."

"Stop with that shit right the fuck now," he interrupts me. My hand covers his mouth to keep him from talking.

"Listen to me, please." A playful side comes out of him because he does the last thing I expect him to. He nips the palm of my hand with his teeth, then licks me as well. Jesus, this man is a hazard to my panties. "Can I talk now?" I smile when he nods his head. Griff could have taken my hand away at any moment, but he chose not to, and that shows me how much he cares. "I'm not saying it to talk down to myself. Believe me, I'm not. You've given me so many gifts, and not monetary either. It's the way you take care of me. I go to bed each night knowing you'll be there when I wake up. You've stood by my side when no one else would have. Griff, you rescued me when the two people I should have been able to trust were going to let me faint and fall flat on my face. One day, I'm going to pay you back. I'm not sure how, but I will."

"Babe, you give me more than you know. Sweet hellos, dinner cooked, my boy being taken care of without hesitation, soft *daddy's*, you in my clothes. Stormy, this isn't a give or take or who's done more than the other." Finn chooses that moment to make his presence known, jumping on the couch, inserting himself between the two of us. The sadness disappears, and all I can do is laugh.

"Oh, Finn, you can't handle not having all of the attention." I pet his head while my other hand cups Griff's jaw. "And thank you for more than you'll ever know." My head descends, needing to have one more taste of Griff, especially right now. His hand slides up my back, fingers tangling in my hair. I may have started the kiss, but make no mistake about it, Griff is already taking control. He holds me where he wants me, his other hand firm on my hip. I rock my body, unable to hold back on what he does to me. His tongue meets mine, tangling with one another, in a role where he dominates mine.

"Fuck." He pulls away from me, forehead meeting mine as the alarm on his phone goes off, an interruption that neither of us is welcoming. Our kiss is abandoned as well as the possibility of us going further.

"How does the saying go? Distance makes the heart grow fonder?" I joke. My laugh doesn't sound very convincing even to myself. We were so close to taking this a lot further, at least I was. Though it doesn't take much when Griff is near—one kiss, a graze of his fingers along my skin, or even a glance.

"I still don't like leaving you. Jack's number is in your phone, right?" he asks, standing up and planting my feet on the ground. I back up. Finn has already moved away in order not to get trampled on.

"It's in my phone. Mom and Aunt Cat know you're leaving and will be around. I'll be fine. You're worrying over nothing when it's me who should be worrying over you." I'm holding back how stressed I am that Griff is going into a situation where sure, he's the rescuer, but roles could be reversed in an instant.

"Alright, let me grab my bag. Walk me out?" I nod, trying to clear my head of thoughts of him getting injured on the job. Shit, his lip is finally healing, and the bruise on his jaw is going away. I stand where I am, watching him in his gray cotton shirt perfectly molded to his muscular back, his ass encased in jeans that have been washed so many time they're soft to the touch. I must have been in my own world watching his slow gait, each flex and pull of his muscle, enjoying my view when Griff gets my attention. "Stormy, you gonna walk me out?" His signature smirk is what I'm met with when I finally peel my eyes away from his body.

"Coming! Finn, let's go see daddy off," I call out for him. He's fast on his feet, the clicking of his nails against the tile floor the only reason I can hear him.

"Jesus, baby girl, I'm never going to leave now." Finn and I meander toward Griff. He's got his duffle bag in one hand, keys and phone in the other.

"Nope, off you go. Finn and I are going to the dog store later. Then we are going to enjoy our long walks along the beach, maybe eat some watermelon together, and then cuddle on the couch." Griff shakes his head. When I meet him at the door leading the garage, I follow him out. One step at a time, he may not know it yet, but he's taking a piece of my heart with him.

"Keep him out of our bed, baby girl."

"I can't make any promises," I reply. He hits the button on the key fob, starting his truck. My car is in the garage stall next to his looking at me longingly because she hasn't gotten a lot of use since moving in. I follow him to the driver's side door, watching as he throws his bag on the passenger seat. His wallet comes out of his back pocket, and he puts the rest of his stuff in the center console.

"I'll promise you this, if I come home and Finn thinks he can sleep on my side of the bed or with my woman permanently, it'll be my palm you feel against your ass," he says, spinning around.

"I'm not sure if that's a threat. I kind of like the idea of that." He steps into my space, engulfing me with his presence, surrounding me in the way only Griff can.

"We'll see about that when you can't sit for a week without the reminder of my palm coming down on your bare ass." He dips his body, lowers his head to my ear. His tongue flicks at the lobe and sets off a tingling deep within my body.

"Griff." My hands come up to his chest, pulling at his shirt until he's as close as possible.

"Fuck, wish I had more time." His lips graze my cheek until they are on mine. One kiss will never be enough. He must have the same realization because it's over all too soon, but there's a shit ton of meaning behind the soft and sweet kiss.

"Be safe. Text me when you get there, and I'll see you soon." We pull away, he gives Finn a pat on his head, and then he's swinging his body into his truck.

"Soon," he says right before he closes the truck door. Finn and I stay where we are until he's pulling out of the garage. We walk together, me waving as he finishes backing out, staying where I'm at until his truck is no longer visible. I take a deep breath, dropping the façade of being strong for a moment. Finn must realize my somber mood because he nudges my thigh, getting my attention.

"Yeah, let's go for a walk on the beach," I tell him, then turn around and walk back into the house, where I know we'll be met with the absence of Griff. Maybe if I keep us super busy, we won't miss the man of the house too much. Probably wishful thinking, but it's better than wallowing in sadness.

18

GRIFFIN

"Goddamn, it's been too long," I tell Stormy on the screen of my phone. Yesterday, I sent her a text that I'd made it. She responded with a picture of her and Finn on the beach. I put my phone away, went over the itinerary, how many boats would be in the water, and the course we'd be working. It was work and nothing but work until I crawled into bed, my head hit the pillow, and I was out like a light. I'd have texted or called her if the early hours of the morning weren't creeping as it is by the time, I got away from everyone the clock laughed in my face, she'd be fast asleep that I wasn't waking her up even with a message.

"Good morning to you, too. It's been less than twenty-four hours. Are you admitting that you miss me?" She is in our bed, the covers pulled up to her shoulders, and I don't miss the flash of yellow behind her. Christ, Finn is going to take my spot all too easily if I'm out of town more than I already am.

"I've got no shame admitting that I miss you, Stormy." Her face gets soft, this time not from sleep, since I more than likely woke her up with the early phone call.

"I miss you, too, Griff." She props her phone up on the nightstand. The comforter moves away from her body. A groan leaves me at seeing the shirt of mine she's wearing. This one white, nearly thread bare, and I can see the outline of her nipples. What I wouldn't give to be with her right now. I already know where I'd start, too. I'd take one pebbled peak, sucking it through the fabric, while my hand would slide up the back of her thigh, wedging myself between her spread legs. I'd repeat the process with her other nipple until the cotton shirt is nice and wet, much like I know her cunt would be. The cool air and damp shirt would do what my mouth couldn't as I moved down her body. It wouldn't take me long to work my way to her cunt. Fuck, I can practically taste it, and we're hundreds of miles away from one another. Christ, I'd take this a whole lot further if it weren't for the fact that I'm rooming with another person in this small home that's been rented for us to use. As it is, someone could walk in and interrupt, which wouldn't be an issue on my end, but I'll be damned if someone hears or sees Stormy in mid-orgasm, or fucking forbid if she were stripped naked. I'd lose my Goddamn mind.

"Griff, you're a million miles away. I won't keep you. I know you've got a lot going on and need to prepare for." I break out of my thoughts. If she only fucking knew what was going on in my head.

"I'm good. Work is the last thing on my mind right now." It should be the first, especially with the situations we deal with. At any given moment, a boat could wreck by taking the wrong turn or hitting a wave at just the right angle. The fuel they carry makes it even more dangerous.

"Oh, really." Her bare legs appear in my screen, and I'm left biting back another groan. Maybe I should have canceled this job after all. My head is not in the game. It's buried in everything that's Stormy.

"Baby girl, the things I'd do to you if this

house weren't full of men who could interrupt us at any given moment." Fuck this, being away from Stormy is not my idea of a good time. Next time I'm at a boat race, I'll make sure we get our own place. Four nights away from my woman is going to turn me into a bigger asshole than I already am with the others around. At least if she's here each night, I know I'll be coming back to her. There won't be a seven-hour drive home, making it impossible to be home right after the last race on Sunday. Four nights away from her is too damn long.

"Griff, that's not fair." She moves again, this time sitting off to the side, unknowingly giving me a glance of her bare pussy. Stormy listens, even when I'm not home.

I look over my shoulder, see no one is near the door, stand up from my place on the too small bed, close the door, and lock it for good measure. "Lift your shirt for me, baby girl. I need something to tide me over." I walk back to my phone. It's propped up on a pillow, my bulge front and center giving Stormy a view of my own. These damn cargo pants do more than hold supplies; they're giving my woman a show for her to see exactly what she does to me.

"Oh God, time better fly because there is no way I'm going to be able to keep my hands to myself," she admits while gathering the hem of my white shirt in her fingers. I watch as each inch of skin is bared to me, smooth and silky. My fists clench and unclench. Never a-fucking-gain am I going out of town without her, mark my words.

"You touch your pussy while I'm not there or on the phone with you, we're going to have problems," I grunt as she shows me her bare pussy, lips glistening with wetness, and damn if I don't wish I were there to wrap my lips around her pretty little clit.

"Then you can't take care of yourself either. Fair is fair," she replies. Little minx. I don't respond, too busy watching as she keeps lifting her shirt up until her tits are in my view.

"Goddamn it, I should have canceled this weekend." In no way was I prepared to be away from her this soon. "And, baby girl, you don't have to worry about me taking my fist to my cock, remembering how you look at this exact moment." Her breath hitches, legs tremble while she presses her thighs together. Damn, this is going to kill us both. It's going to take everything I have not to pull up this memory when I'm in the shower late tonight and paint my cum on the shower walls. I readjust myself, take one last glance at Stormy. Her hair is tousled from sleep, cheeks flush with color either from sleep or being turned on. I'm going with the latter. She's standing there with my shirt up to her damn neck, tits firm and a handful, nipples tight like rosebuds, hourglass figure where her stomach slopes inwards before flaring out to her hips. Hips that I love leaving my fingerprints on from holding her while I fuck her. Even when she's riding me, it's me lifting her up and pulling her down. No way do I allow Stormy to do the work, and fuck if she doesn't like it.

"Christ, my baby girl is so Goddamn beautiful," I tell her.

"Yo, Griffin, we gotta roll out!" A knock interrupts our time together. Exactly why I didn't take this a step further. It'd be just our luck her fingers would be buried inside her tight cunt, and she'd be on the edge of coming. My cock would be in my hand, fucking myself as she does the same, and this shit would happen.

"Be right there!" I tell one of the guys through the door. Each race, it's a different team, so there's no telling which one is which, not that I give a single fuck at this moment.

"You've got to go," Stormy says, worry in her tone.

"Yeah, baby girl, I do. You take care of my boy and stay out of trouble," I tell her, not doing anything to alleviate her worry. There's no reason to talk about what-ifs.

"Of course. Stay safe and come back in one piece. No more busted lips or bruised jaws from any job, please." A smile tugs at my lips. This woman, she's got me wrapped around her damn finger.

"I will. See you soon. I'm not sure I'll have a chance to call again, but I'll text you." Stormy swallows, nodding her response.

"Griff, man, we gotta go. They're in the truck waiting." I hear another knock, and I know it's not the time to say what I want. It'll have to wait until I get home and have Stormy in my arms.

"Promise, Stormy. I'll be okay."

"Go. Don't worry about me. I'm being ridiculous. Talk to you soon." This time, she's more together with her emotions.

"Talk soon." I hang up the phone, grab it from its place on my bed, and head for the door. I'm re-thinking a lot of fucking things, this job being one of them. It doesn't give me the adrenaline rush it once did. My thoughts are wrapped up in Stormy. I'm wishing the fucking days away until I'm back home with her, and right now, the last thing I need to be doing is thinking. I need to get into work mode, stat.

19

GRIFFIN

This fucking weekend can't be over fast enough. There hasn't been a moment with this crew that's felt natural. The guys are younger. Fucking idiots is what they are. They love to hear themselves talk about the rescues they've done and the tail they pick up when the day is over. Their words, not mine. Even if I were in my twenties and single, no damn way I'd be talking about women like they're pieces of meat. I'm just glad today is the final race and the second I'm out of this helicopter and my gear is turned in, I'm out of here. There's no way I'll be going back to the house, getting a few hours of sleep only to leave in the morning. It's not like I've gotten a whole hell of a lot of sleep anyways. We finish our day, they go out, I grab a quick bite to eat, and head to my room. The only thing I want to do is talk to Stormy for a while, grab a shower, and pass out only to start over again. I'd no sooner fall asleep only to be woken up from them coming in for the night, running into walls, laughing it up, drunk off their asses. The trust you have in your crew is gone when you realize they're working while hungover the next day and it's been repeated each night. Specifically last night. I was on the phone with Stormy when she heard the shitbags come in, and I saw the worry on her face through our FaceTime call. It took me a few minutes to calm her down, but the die was cast, and I know she wasn't going to sleep well afterwards. Maybe it is time to hang up doing these side jobs. No amount of money is worth an accident to occur because your crew is worthless. I text Stormy one last time to let her know my plans.

> Me: See you tomorrow. Keep the bed warm for me. I'm leaving as soon as we're done here.

I hit the send button, drop my phone in my dry bag we keep on the helicopter, and get to work. No sooner we're up in the sky, my eyes are on the water and the first race is under way. Things have been going smoothly with the boats and races, almost too smoothly. There's never not been an incident each time I work on a race, and I know it's still too early to have a quiet day. I watch the second race; this one has my hackles raised. The boat in the left lane is choppier, not under control compared to the boat on the right side. I'm ready to rock and roll when I see one boat hit a wave at the right angle and go airborne, hitting the other.

"It's go-time," I hear Smith say in my ear. I block him out unless it's necessary to communicate. Hopefully fucking never again after this weekend. I'm ignoring him. Its' me and the rescue mission. Not the dumb fuck who thinks he's got everything under control.

"Damn it," I mutter under my breath, watching as the racer is ejected into the water. "Get up," I tell him silently, hoping he's able to recover without needing a rescue. He's not, and that means it's time for me to go.

"Hawk, you're up," Smith says in the comm we have in our ears. He's shortened my last name from Hawkins to Hawk, and while it doesn't bother me, the fucker acts like we've been friends when that's the last thing he is to me. I heard the snickers and the bullshit talking about me being locked in my room. Biting my tongue and not knocking him off his ass was hard. The dumb fuck probably has nothing waiting for him at home with that mentality.

"10-4." I get myself locked in, ready for them to lower me down in the water. Matt has already been lowered to work on a patient, and now I'm being sent to work on the other. The guy is face first in the water, not moving, which isn't the greatest situation, but it could be worse. Him not wearing a life jacket is one of those. Some of these guys think they're invincible, which they'd have to, going over one hundred sixty miles per hour. Goddamn these crazy bastards.

Smith lowers me. My hands stay clear of the trail tine. The cable that comes down from the helicopter is charged with static electricity, and I'm not trying to get injured. I'm hovering above the water, ready to disconnect at a moment's notice. Adrenaline is pumping through my veins, worried about an explosion that could and will happen. The fuel running in race boats is high octane and highly flammable. My feet hit the water, and it's time for me to get to work. I disconnect from my line, leaving it swinging in the wind.

My arms pull and push through the water, legs kicking to move as swiftly without using too much of my energy while swimming toward the patient. The ocean isn't for the weak, that's for sure. I'm a few feet away when I notice the man is still face down, completely unconscious. The lack of oxygen has me kicking into high gear until I get to him, immediately flipping him onto his back while treading water.

"If you can hear me, this is Griff Hawkins," I tell the racer even though I know he's down for the count. Blood is gushing from his face. My hand goes to his neck, feeling for a pulse while I wait for Smith to bring the basket down. That's how it goes—you lower the medic, disconnect, bring the line back up, and hook the basket in, and then the racer is lifted. Another boat will come around and pick me up while they assess the patient in whether he can be taken care of by the crew or needs to be flown to a hospital. What feels like a lifetime later, I see the basket being lowered from the helicopter. Too fucking long, which means these asshats aren't on their A-game.

"I'm going to lift you in the basket," I tell my patient, who has a thready heart rate and shallow breathing. Most of the time, there'd be another guy in the water with me, but since there's another racer who needed help, it meant going solo. I swim the short distance to the basket, one arm around the patient, my lightweight life jacket allowing me to work easily.

"We're going to take good care of you, buddy," I tell him. His eyes still aren't open, and it doesn't take me long to hoist him into the basket before lifting myself up. Only things don't go as planned. I'm almost in when the helicopter dips. I look up, unable to use my comm at the moment. I wouldn't be able to hear them, and they wouldn't be able to hear me over the blades. Another dip occurs, and the grasp I have on the basket is lost. I'm a tangle of limbs trying to keep the patient steady while maintaining my own balance, but it's too fucking late. A tailspin happens, I'm falling backwards, and instead of holding on, I let go, unwilling to let the patient feel anything more than he already has. Karma or luck, whatever the fickle bitch wants to be, is not on my side. The basket comes charging back at me, and I've got barely enough time to get my face out of the way. My shoulder takes the brunt of the weight, and then I'm going down.

"Goddamn it!" Fire consumes me, and I'm

left seeing stars. The last thing I see is the helicopter maintaining its balance, finally, and the basket making its way up. After that, I close my eyes and brace for impact. The only thing going to break my fall is the water. Even still, it's a long way to go. A vision of Stormy pissed as fuck, ready to kick ass and take names is what I'm holding on to when I plunge into the deep water. My feet are already kicking, the life jacket doing its job and helping propel me upwards. My non-injured hand goes up in the air. The medic boat crew will see me with the other spotters. One thing's for sure: I'm hanging my hat up with this shit. I can feel the dislocation in my shoulder, and that's going to be a bitch to explain to Stormy. It'll be even harder to hide wearing a damn sling for however long it'll take to heal.

A boat approaches me while I bop in the water. A sitting duck in an ocean full of sharks isn't my idea of fun, and I'm thankful they're not delaying like that fuck Smith.

"You okay?" a man asks when the boat is close enough.

"Shoulder took the brunt of it, but I'm fine." More pissed off than anything else. He lowers the ladder on the backside of the boat, and I couldn't be more fucking thankful.

"Yeah, that shit was not easy to watch." He can say that again.

"Appreciate you picking me up. You got a medic on board?" I ask, using my good arm to help propel me up.

"We do, but it'll have to wait. We need to get out of here, and quick." It's then I see the fire licking at the wrecked boats. Racing fuel is going to make things go boom quickly. I nod my response, take a seat in an open one, and we're racing against time until the boats will explode.

"No problem. Probably better to have this taken a look at by a doctor before paperwork needs to be done," I say more for myself, but the other guy shakes his head in disgust, more than likely over the paperwork. Meanwhile, I'm wondering how I'm going to explain what happened to Stormy while simultaneously keeping her calm. Good fucking luck with that. So much for getting home tonight. The amount of red tape will guarantee that won't be happening. I'll be lucky to call or text her. My phone is in that helicopter, and if the way the helicopter was handled is anything to go by, well, I may as well kiss it goodbye.

20

STORMY

The past few days have sucked. Griff and I have been missing each other, not just emotionally either. Believe me, I am there. Never in my life did I think I'd miss a man as much as I miss him. Nope, he'd miss my text, I'd miss his call, and him leaving a voicemail didn't alleviate the longing. Instead, I saved it, replaying it at night before going to bed in order to hear his voice. I didn't leave him a voicemail back. I sent a video of Finn and myself on the couch saying we can't wait for Monday. Even if I'm lying through my teeth. Not about Griff coming home, but for me, it means I've got to face work and really set foot back in town.

"Dang it, Finn. We missed Griff again," I talk to the fluffy Golden Retriever out loud, seeing the text from the man himself. When Finn woke up at his standard time, I groaned in protest. The sleep I hoped for to come last night didn't happen. There was no amount of reading to make me tired enough either. I tossed and turned so much even Finn left the comfort of the bed, choosing his place on the couch instead. I nab my phone, hit the reply button, and send him a text.

Me: I can't wait. See you soon.

Finn barks, making his displeasure known. Whether it's about Griff remains unknown. It is his kibble time, so I'm sure that's the reason.

"Alright, I'll get your food ready, then my coffee." I go the fridge to pull out the sliced-up fruit I've been adding to Finn's dry dog food, my creamer, and then go to the pantry to finish off his breakfast. Griff says I spoil him. I don't agree. Finn was spoiled long before I came along. The only difference is, now he's living a healthier lifestyle with more walks.

The clanging of the dog food and fruit hits the metal bowl. Finn sits like the king he is until I give him the words he's used to. "Good boy." He gives me his paw, and then he's chowing down. I leave him to his morning ritual and head to the coffee pot, trying to figure out what we should do today. Groceries are ready for the week, the house is clean, and I've been slowly unpacking my things to set around the house. My books are now in the once sparse wood built-ins, a natural wood tone like a lot of the furniture Griff has in his house, well, our house. It's not the usual white and blue style house you see in most beach houses. It's homey, lived in, and relaxed. Which is probably why my books came out of the boxes faster than I intended them to. I was worried this wouldn't last, but those are unfounded. Seriously, Griff has shown me in more than one what it's like to truly be cared for in the terms of a stable man. My father obviously wasn't one of those, and Zach, well, you see what happens when you settle.

I make my cup of coffee, put a healthy dose of creamer in Griff's mug. One that has Finn's face plastered all over it. A gift from Jack on Father's Day, the year he picked up Finn.

"Maybe I'll call Mom and see what she's up to today." I blow the steam out of my coffee mug before taking my first sip. I make my way out of the kitchen and walk through the living room. Seeing my things mingled with Griff's hits me deep inside my chest. My feather display is the only thing that needs to be put on the shelf, and since it needs to go on the top, I'm shit out of luck. Even with a kitchen chair I can't reach, and no way am I going to try and lug the ladder inside from the garage only to smash the ceiling fan.

I continue my walk, hearing Finn come up beside me, so I open the back door, and he wedges his way out first. "How rude. Someone is forgetting their manners." Another plus with all my infinite amount of time while not working is at least I've got Finn to keep me company, and I'm not completely bat shit crazy talking to myself. It's not like he responds to the crazy, could still be up for debate, but this way, I'm not inundating Mom and Aunt Cat to keep me busy. Finn wanders off, and I take my seat under the covered patio. An overhead fan spins above, doing a smidgen of good in the heat and humidity. I'd like to say after summer, it cools down a lot, but the truth of the matter is, it's not until mid-fall that we see a cooler temperature.

I tuck myself into one of the cushioned

chairs, drink my coffee, and stare off at the ocean. In another hour or so, the beach will start filling up, chatter will be carried through the sand dunes, the tips of canopies will make it hard to see the waves hitting the shore, and one day, I hope it's us down there with a family of our own.

"Finn, what are you doing, crazy boy?" He's running through the yard in circles, getting his zoomies out of the way. It's funny the way he'll run and run and run only to pass out ten minutes later. Literally, the big lug won't move from his spot for hours, not even when a delivery man is at the door. Finn settles next to my feet once he's done, and if we don't get inside, he'll demand to stay our here forever. That's not happening once the sun fully peaks and the hottest part of the day hits. "Come on, boy, it's time to go inside." I take another couple of sips of my coffee, knowing one cup is my limit, and if I make a second cup, it'll sit on the counter, cold. We head back inside, for the couch, Finn in one corner, me in the other as I stretch my legs out. I've soon got the television on some reality train wreck of a show, the blanket is thrown over my body, and I'm drifting to sleep.

A SHRILL of laughter wakes me up from a dead sleep. I look everywhere thinking someone is in the house only to realize it was the television. My eyes are still adjusting to the light, which is a lot dimmer than what I expected. Finn has moved closer to me, burrowing under the blanket, and is breathing on my calf. I wouldn't be surprised if he's been snoring.

"Fuck," I mumble. The sun is low, and I've slept all freaking day. Finn lifts his head as I scramble off the couch. Griff is supposed to be home sometime tonight, and I'd at least like to have dinner cooked in case he comes back hungry. I'm looking for my phone, not remembering where I left it earlier this morning. My bladder screams at me in protest, and Finn is now up, pacing back and forth. I run to the sliding glass door and fling it open, not wanting to have to clean up two accidents. I leave it open, run through the kitchen, see my phone on the counter, and snatch it up.

"Shit, shit, shit." I've got a missed call from Griff along with three texts sent in succession an hour ago.

Griff: Going to be late getting home.

Griff: Never mind. It's going to be tomorrow. I'm stuck doing paperwork because of an incident.

Griff: Baby girl, you okay?

The last one came a while after the second text, and Griff knows I'm by my phone, especially after we met. I forget about needing to use the bathroom, immediately hitting Griff's number, praying I'll get an answer. The knowledge that I won't is at the forefront of my mind. If he's got a problem going on, the last thing he's going to do is answer. The call rings, once, twice, three times, and then goes to voicemail. He's obviously busy. I hit the end button. Ugh, I'm so pissed at myself. The need to not be clingy is thrown out the window.

Me: I'm sorry I missed your call. Please tell me everything is okay and call me later if you get a chance. Finn and I were taking a nap. I now understand why he loves the couch so much <3

Griff doesn't respond, and that sucks even

more. This time, I keep my phone on me, even though I'm going to use the bathroom. The damn thing will be glued to my hand from now until eternity.

21

STORMY

Today is the day for two reasons. First, Griff comes home. Thankfully, we spoke for a few minutes last night. He was vague but assured me he was okay and he'd be heading home first thing this morning as soon as they were released. The other reason is I'm back to work, and my schedule is full for my first day back at the salon.

"Hey, honey, you ready to open up?" Kitty, the store owner, asks after we've had a cup of coffee and set up our stations for the day. Today is absolutely a two-cup minimum, if not a third by the way of an iced coffee from the shop next door. I woke up extra early, made sure Finn was taken care of, then took a longer walk than our usual. He must have realized it, too, because I got an extra dose of puppy dog eyes when I grabbed my bag while saying goodbye to the big couch potato.

"As ready as I'll ever be, I suppose." My stomach is a riot house. I guess it's a good thing one of my first clients is a regular. Marie's hair is a root touch-up and a trim, every six weeks like clockwork, unless she changes things up. So far, it's been the same honey-blonde hair for the past few years.

"It's been two weeks. Surely, the dust has settled and someone else will become more interesting," Kitty says, walking to the door and unlocking it. I move in the same direction, pulling on the string that signals we're open in a bright pink neon sign that reads Kitty's Style and Wash. Only time will tell on what I'll be dealing with. The only thing certain is that time marches on. Eventually. I was really hoping to see Griff this morning before heading to work, to soak in some of his confidence, even if it were only a hug. That didn't happen, and I'm not holding it against him. I probably shouldn't even use him as a crutch, but tell that to my nerves.

"I guess we'll see. At least Marie is my first

client." Maybe she won't bring anything up, and we can have a normal day.

"That's good. It's been boring without you here. Promise me you won't take another two weeks off." I snort. I'm not fun by any means. Kitty probably missed me opening or closing when she needed some time off and knows I'm the most reliable.

"Oh, I can assure you there will be no time off in my future. I'm actually thinking about opening my books a weekend a month," I admit, not going into full detail on the reason why.

"You've got a key, honey. Do what you need to, but don't overwork yourself," she says before dashing to the back of the salon, probably to bring out a load of towels that need to be washed.

The door chimes, alerting me to a guest. Marie walks in saying, "Hey, Stormy."

"Hey, girlfriend, you're looking fabulous as ever." I'm back at my station, going through my products and making sure none of the other stylists have snatched them up. There's a rule that stylist can borrow things from one another, but you're supposed to return it. Ask me if that'll actually happens.

"Oh no, ma'am, honey, that would be you. You're absolutely glowing." A genuine smile plasters on my face. After sleeping all day, I needed a shower. It was time for me to get back into my Sunday routine. Self-care, if you would —exfoliate, shave everything, deep-conditioning mask, and then washing my hair was in the works. Once that was done, I made a quick bite to eat. A girl-style dinner, unhealthy to its core. A bag of chips and salsa was exactly what I wanted, and I was eating my feelings. By the time I was done eating, it was time to blow dry my hair, my phone on the bathroom counter, face up just in case, and Finn on the floor beside me. It's a good thing I brought my phone with me. I was halfway done blowing my hair out when Griff called. I'd never been more ecstatic to hear his voice even with not-so-fun news.

"Thank you, I'm going to take the compliment even though I'm sure it was my time on the beach that helped." I pat the seat for Marie to come over so we can get started.

"Sure, we'll go with that." Marie winks, and I blush. Griff and I aren't hiding, but we're not telling everyone our business. They can figure things out for themselves or ask. My name has been through the mud one too many times for me to allow others to demean it some more.

"Are we doing the usual?" I ask, placing a cape around her, snapping it at the back of her neck. I run my fingers through her hair, look at the new growth coming in, and mentally remember the formula I use with her.

"We are. I think the next appointment, I want to switch it up. There's no use keeping up with the gray hair when it's only getting worse, and I'm only getting older." My hands meet one another, clapping excitedly. Marie has been talking about this for a while, going back and forth. The things I want to do to her hair, and this way, we can make it more natural instead of just growing it out.

"I can hear your excitement in the back." Kitty comes out in an apron.

"Marie is going gray. Have you seen a head of hair prettier?" I reply.

"And with your magical hands, it's going to be magnificent," Kitty responds as the door chimes again. I don't bother looking, figuring it's another client for one of the other stylists who haven't come in yet.

"Okay, so if you're positive, I'm going to do a demi-permanent color, then we can strip the rest of the color next appointment." Marie nods vigorously, so I continue, "You're looking at a few hours. Bring a book, wear comfortable clothes, and we'll order food." She'll be my only client that day. It'll be hours of standing, watching, and waiting.

"I can't wait. I should have planned ahead. We could have done it today." She shrugs her shoulders, and Marie probably could have called me if I hadn't turned my work calls onto silent mode. Shit on a brick.

"That's okay. This appointment won't take long. Let me go get your color mixed up, and we'll get started." I squeeze her shoulders once, turn around, and am stopped in my tracks. The door chiming brought in an unwelcome guest: Zach's mother, Laura. I push my shoulders back and lift my chin, pretending I've got all the confidence in the world when I walk by the salon chair she's sitting in. Her stylist, Cassidy, isn't here yet, but leave it to Laura to talk on the phone as loudly as possible. "That's what I said. She's living with her best friend's uncle. Can you imagine leaving my son on his wedding day with a man who's closer to her mom's age than hers?" *She's not worth it, she's not worth it, she's absolutely not worth it.* The mantra replays in my head the entire walk toward the back room, while I'm flinging open cabinets, slamming them shut, mixing product, and everyone leaves me alone while I get my emotions in check. Jesus, I could really use Griff right about now, or a bottle of tequila. In either order. Or for someone to put Laura in her place. I take a deep breath, abandoning mixing the color to try and get my shit in check. The last thing I want is for Laura to see she's affecting me. That bitch and her son are my past, and there's no use looking in the rearview mirror.

22

GRIFFIN

"Hey, Jack." I hit the button to answer the call in my truck. They released us at midnight last night after going through each person with a fine-tooth comb. My questioning was done at a hospital. It wasn't the first time I'd dislocated my shoulder, and the doctor was unimpressed it happened again. He warned me that a surgery could be in my future. I knew it. With my field, it comes with the territory. The doctor told me all of this while putting my shoulder back in place, the pain of it hanging loosely only for him to put me in even more pain when it's finally where it belongs.

"Hey, you home yet?" he asks.

"About five minutes out. Going to drop my

shit off, let Finn out, and pick up some food to bring to Stormy at the salon." I heard the longing in her voice on the three-minute phone call. It ate at my gut. It's why I drove a couple of hours, hit a rest area, ate ibuprofen like it was candy, took a nap, and woke up to finish the drive home. Yesterday was a cluster-fuck of all clusterfucks, one I won't be repeat-ing. The first call I made was to my boss, the one who didn't show up yesterday and was supposed to, especially after the incident. Marty tried to give me the run-around, like he was blowing smoke up my skirt. It came down to me say get fucked. He shut up. I told him I was done, this time for good, and hung up.

"Head to the salon first. Laura is there and hot to trot," Jack replies.

"Don't you worry about Stormy. I'm on my way to the salon now. Laura Busby doesn't know who she's messed with. I'm going to make her wish she hadn't stepped foot in Kitty's salon. That bitch has never gone there before, yet today she's there. I think the fuck not," Barbie is going on in the background. I'm already steering my truck in the opposite direc-tion, taking a side street until my tires hit the red brick in the town square.

"Barbie, I've got it covered. I'm pulling into

a parking spot now. We all know she's not gonna say dick when I'm around."

"That's just the tip of it, Griff. Mel and Zach are back in town. I imagine it's going to get worse before it gets better." Christ on a mother-fucking cracker. It's Monday, and everything is falling to shit.

"Don't worry about Melissa. I'll straighten her spoiled as up, too," Barbie hollers again. I've got to hand it to her. When Barbie brings you into the fold, it's for good. She'll fight fire with fire until the bitter end.

"Shit, Mel won't survive Barbie, you know that, right?" I tell Jack.

"That's what I'm afraid of. Melissa has a lot coming to her, and I'm not wading in this shit." Better Jack than me. Mel is a grown-ass woman. She knows better, and he can't fix this for her.

"Gotta go. My woman is being ambushed. Keep Barbie at the bar, tell her I'll be back tomorrow. And why don't you quit holding your dick in your hand? It's time for you to go after what you want." I shift the gear into *Park*, slamming it into place with my good shoulder.

"Keep me posted, and I'm trying. If you ever tried to tame a wild horse, you'd understand that Barbie is making me work for it." I chuckle at the analogy. He's not wrong. She's her own person, been alone for many years, is a hardass with a soft side. It's getting to the middle that'll take Jack some time.

"Will do. Good luck." I hit the end button without saying goodbye again. It's Jack; he'll get over it. And I'm sure I'll get another call from him later on. I've been driving for hours, my shoulder is in a sling, and I could sleep for a damn week. I grab my phone and wallet from the center console, managing to put my leather bifold in my back pocket. My keys and phone can stay in my hand. That way, if I have something to keep me busy, I won't get twitchy and do something I'll regret.

I'm a block away on foot from the salon. Most of the parking spots were full. Tourist season makes it impossible to get closer, which is alright. Maybe I'll cool off. I can only imagine what Laura is spewing. Her mouth was awful quick to say that Stormy and I were having an affair. We gave her a fuck lot to talk about, but it wouldn't have hurt her to ask a question or two. I don't know, maybe ask her son the reason why his bride was running for the door without a backward glance. Laura's the reason Stormy didn't get out of the house for nearly a week, and when she did, well, I was the lucky one she graced with her presence. I knew I had a good thing going with her from the moment she was in my truck and she was clutching the bottles of tequila. Most women would go after champagne. That's not Stormy, though; she likes her alcohol with a little bite.

I nod my head to a few people I see as I walk the sidewalk. The coffee shop is busy; a line is out the door for people to get their fix of caffeine. Damn good thing I'll be heading home after I make sure Stormy is okay. The need for coffee of my own is strong, and since I take mine black with one sugar, I don't see the point in paying four dollars for one. A few more paces, and I'm opening the door to Kitty's place. The noise from the blow dryers and chatters stops right away. I don't see Stormy anywhere. What I do see is Laura on the phone. Her face pales, and it seems like I've come to save my woman at the right time. The door closes behind me. The air conditioning hums in the quiet. What I'm waiting on is for Stormy to appear.

"Hey, Griffin," Kitty greets me, head tilting to the back of the shop. I'm just about to head in that direction when my woman appears. She stops in her tracks, barely holding on to what

I'm sure is some kind of color. Her hair is down, raven locks cascading in soft waves. A light dusting of makeup. Stormy steals the air from my lungs with one damn look. It doesn't matter if she's wearing my clothes, a bathing suit, or what she has on now—a black form-fitting top, loose jeans with her lower abdomen showing, and sandals on her feet.

"Griff, my God, what happened?" I'm going to answer that, but first, I'm going to make a woman run out of the salon with her tail between her legs. If I don't do it, Barbie will, and Laura will be more than scared. She'll hightail it to the nearest cop to make a false report. Then Barbie would make good on her promise, bat in tow like she's Harley Quinn from *Suicide Squad*.

23

STORMY

Oh my God, oh my freaking God. I'm barely holding on by a thread. The two cups of coffee I had are threatening to come up with the emotions swirling through my body. Griff is standing in front of me, which isn't out of the ordinary even though he wasn't supposed to be back this early. It's the dark circles beneath his eyes, the scruff he usually keeps trimmed that's now untamed, and the fucking sling holding his arm up. I should have known something was up. My radar should have set me off.

He keeps his eyes on me for a moment, allowing me to soak in his presence. If only he'd move his feet, or I'd move mine. The two of us don't stand still. My tears cloud my view, and I blink them away so they don't roll down my cheeks. Griff must be over this self-imposed stand-off, because he makes it one step before he changes direction.

"No, no, no," I mumble so low it's barely a whisper, worry hitting me for a different reason now. He walks closer to Laura. She's in her own world. Oblivious to the hulking man walking up to her.

"Oh, this is going to be good, honey. It's been a long time in the making." Kitty comes up beside me, takes the color out of my hand, and plops it on a tray. A good thing, too, with the way I'm trembling on the inside.

"I don't want her to retaliate on Griff, his bar, his name, all because of me," I admit. The Busby's have enough money and clout to make people's life a living hell, a feeling I know all too well.

"A man like Griffin Hawkins knows exactly how to handle a woman of that caliber. You just stay here with me, let him do the Lord's work." Her hand catches mine, squeezing it once. Cassidy opens the door, hitting the doorstopper with her foot to prop the glass door open. We've found we get more tourists coming and going on the footpath, and they love the products Kitty keeps stocked as well as a few accessories. Today, I wish she had forgotten that little task. It's Monday and exceptionally busy. Everyone is getting their last bit of summer fun out of the way before school is back in session and our town settles in for fall.

"You got a problem with Stormy and me?" I hear Griff ask. My eyes close, and I take a deep breath. Of course, she has a problem. The woman can't open her eyes and see two feet in front of her.

"I certainly do. You and that harlot left the wedding. She disgraced my son, and you, well, you should know better. A businessman such as yourself, you've got an image to uphold." I have to put my hand to my mouth, trying to absorb the giggle taking root. Jesus, an image to uphold. Has she met Griff? He doesn't give two shits what others think about him. Griff exudes confidence. The bar is successful, and he's a medic in his off-time. Sure, he gets paid for it, but it's not like he needs that job.

"That the reason you're running your trap far and wide because you're grown son can't handle being an adult?" Laura huffs out a breath of air and gets up from her seat. Griff takes a step back, his arm tucking under the sling. He knows she's not done; it's written all over her face.

"Well, I'll be damned if I let someone drag our last name through the mud and her not come out unscathed." The sad truth of the matter is she truly believes that.

"Woman, you have your head so far up your own ass, you can't see fucking daylight. Did you even ask anyone else their side of the story? Zach or Stormy, for example?" She doesn't like him subjecting her to critical thinking.

"Why would I do that? I saw it for myself," Laura states, vehemently.

"Then I'd suggest you talk to your son. You know, the one who went on a honeymoon with Mel, my niece." Griff doesn't mince words. His voice carries through the quiet salon. Everyone can hear him, and I'm sure so can the people who have congregated around the open door. Shit, some of them even stepped inside. I should be embarrassed with the way more of my dirty laundry is being aired out, except I'm not. Griff is doing what I couldn't and wouldn't. The couldn't part is because people chose who to believe, and as much as it pains me to admit it, Laura is right. How we left was pretty damning. Me moving in with him makes it look worse. I wouldn't for simplicity reasons. No one needs to know what happens in my personal life that much in order to make it common knowledge.

"That still doesn't negate to the fact you're a barbarian, dating someone fifteen years younger than you. Why, the scum beneath my shoes is better than you," Laura spits while clutching her pearls. Swear to God, this cliché keeps getting worse and worse.

"Woman, you don't get your ass gone and leave my woman alone, I'll air it all, and I know your husband has a wandering eye and dick. It seems the apple doesn't fall far from the tree." She doesn't like that, not at all. Also, I'd love to know where Griff found out his information because I was not aware of that little tidbit at all. It just goes to show you people truly can hide what they want. The dinners at Zach's family's house seemed normal. A little stuffy for my liking, but nothing out of the ordinary. Zach's dad was always there and attentive, or so it seemed.

All of a sudden, Laura scurries out the door, head held down in shame. I almost feel sorry for her, almost, except for how she's treated me, past, present, and what I'm sure will be the future. What I'm not prepared for is the round of applause in the salon. My eyes that were once on Griff survey the area. People I don't even know are cheering, some are laughing, and I'm still standing in the same place I was when Griff walked in.

"That's the man you marry, honey," Kitty whispers in my ear as she walks away.

"Thanks, Griffin. Cassidy didn't want to schedule her, and I didn't want her in my shop, but money is money. I have a feeling she won't be back. It was probably a one-and-done type of thing anyways." Griff was making his way toward me when Kitty stopped him in his tracks.

"Nothing to thank me for. You think I can steal Stormy away for a minute?" He talks to Kitty like I'm not there. I roll my eyes. Marie is one of the easiest clients I have, and she won't mind a bit.

"Take all the time you need. I'll entertain Marie for a bit." Griff nods, closing down the conversation, and prowls. There's no other way to put it, he's a lion in sheep's clothing, and I'm his willing victim.

"Griff." My voice trembles as he gets closer. There's bruising along his shoulder where his shirt has shifted down, and this is ten times worse than I first thought. "What happened?

Are you okay? Is this the reason you were dealing with paperwork?" The questions come tumbling out in rapid succession, and what does Griff do? He doesn't respond to a single one of them. Instead, he pulls me to his chest with his good arm and holds me. He's injured, yet Griff is consoling me. I'm careful not to jar his arm or shoulder, whichever is hurt, when I wrap my arms around his waist. I close my eyes and breathe him in. His scent of oranges, cedar, and oak settles me down.

"I'm fine, Stormy. Accidents happen every day. This one could have been prevented. Shit went down. I turned in my notice, and I'm not going back. I don't want to get into it just yet. I will tell you my shoulder was dislocated. It wasn't the first time, but I hope like fuck it's the last." He kisses the crown of my head at the end of his explanation, squeezing me one last time. A silent request for me to get it together, I'm sure.

My lips press a kiss against his chest. "I'm so glad you're okay and home." I know he's leaving a lot out. I also know that if he's done with his time as a boat race medic, it means things went really bad.

"Me too, baby girl."

"You need to go home and rest, but don't

think you'll get away with not telling me what happened when it didn't. You're injured enough to be in a sling." He goes to say something, but I cover his mouth with my hand. "Go home, get some sleep. I have stuff set out to make dinner. When I get home, I'll cook, you'll relax, and let me take care of you for a change."

"Who's bossing whom now?" Griff's eyebrows lift. A grin full of mischief is spreading on his face.

"I am. Deal with it." I rock back on my heels with a smile. He's home in one piece, but the man needs a bed, and soon.

"Kiss your man and get back to work." His head descends, nose sliding along mine until I tip my head up, my mouth meeting his pillowy soft lips. If I thought I was getting away with only grazing his lips, I was all wrong. Griff's tongue slides out. A soft whimper leaves me, and he takes over the kiss. I feel his hand holding the back of my head as he deepens the kiss. I've missed this, missed him, his scent, his feel, the way he takes care of me. And I convey it in our kiss, going to the tips of my toes, needing to be as close as possible to him.

"Damn, baby girl." He pulls away first, and I mourn the loss. "I'm leaving now before I walk you to the back room and let you finish giving me one hell of a welcome home."

"Okay, I'll see you at home."

"Fuck yeah, you will." I'm left in a lust-induced fog courtesy of the man I'm falling for, and I'm finding I like that, a lot.

24

STORMY

While everything seems good on the surface after Griff is home, there's something I have yet to tell him. Between my nap and the self-care Sunday, Aunt Catherine called saying she needed to stop by. Of course, I told her to come on over. The news she delivered wasn't what I wanted to hear. For most of the wedding stuff, the deposits covered the potential cancellation of the wedding. Minus the venue, the most expensive part of the stupid farce I didn't want anyways. Who gets married at a country club when you're not even a part of it, but your future husband and his family are? This could have all been avoided if I had put my foot down, telling them both no, instead of putting it on my credit card, which is now maxed out. Zach said he'd help pay for it. I should have known. Aunt Catherine being the woman she is tried to work around paying for the ceremony at a reduced rate. When that didn't work, she went to Laura, asking if there was a way she could talk to the country club. That's probably why she made her appearance today. Instead of being an adult and talking to me or even my aunt, she does this instead. And yes, I'm aware my mom and aunt have put out a lot of fires that the adult in me should have done. I still kept my mouth shut, licked my wounds, and left everyone alone.

At least Mom only helped pay the deposit instead of the whole damn thing. Ten thousand dollars. I don't even have the full amount in my savings account. I'm going to have to come clean and tell Griff eventually. For the time being, I'm going to pay my mom back first. She deserves that money, it's hers, and it was my sheer stupidity to ask for help when I knew I couldn't afford it completely.

Fucking Zach and his empty promises. I shouldn't have believed him. He was all, *'We'll pay it off once we're married. Just put it on your card.'* Why didn't I make Laura foot the bill since that's where she wanted it in the first place? I guess the good news is, everything else is being refunded minus the deposits. Those are long gone, but hey, at least I was only paying for the ceremony. Zach's family was in charge of the reception, which was even more money. I swear to God if she tries to nail me with that bill, I'll find the most expensive attorney, go into even more debt in order not to. Twenty-five-thousand dollars for a reception, fully catered with wait staff, open bar, and flowers out the wazoo.

"There you go, looking as beautiful as ever." I finished Marie up while in my head. She talked while I listened with half an ear and responded, and for the first time in my career, my heart wasn't in it. It's a good thing I can do this in my sleep.

"It looks great, thank you so much." I take the cape off her, then move her hair in a manner so she can see the cut and style.

"You're welcome. I'm sorry you got a show while you were here." Marie would never hold what happened with Laura against me. I still feel like I should apologize.

"There's nothing for you to worry about. She should be ashamed of herself, not you. Keep your chin up and enjoy that hunk of a man who clearly loves you." Marie stands up, hugs me, goes through the motions of paying me, and leaves me with a tip I wasn't expecting. And it wasn't the monetary kind either. I already knew I was falling for Griff, quicker than what society deems is normal. Especially after being the runaway bride in a jilted kind of way. The truth of the matter is, I am falling, hard and fast. If I keep thinking about all this, I'm going to lose my mind. I may as well clean up my area and the floors while I wait for my next client. The broom is already near my station, so I grab it and get to work. My area is done first. Marie only wanted a trim, so it was an easy cleanup. The rest of the ladies still have clients in their seats.

"You okay, honey?" Kitty asks when I move near her.

"I am. Upset that Griff is hurt and he had to fight my battle, but I'm also really freaking happy all the same." For the first time today, I don't think about the mountain of debt or how this is putting me off track in my savings account. If Kitty decides to sell, there are other ways around purchasing the salon besides putting a wad of cash on the table.

"I'm glad for you. Do you have another client coming in shortly?" She's working on a perm on one of her own usuals. That's a lot of arm movement in one day. Kitty is known for her perms with the older ladies and spares us all because of it. I'll do them, but I'd rather not.

"I've got another thirty minutes. I'm thinking about grabbing an iced coffee and a bagel from next door. Want anything?" The last thing I should be doing is spending more money. Tomorrow will be a new day, and I'll pack my lunch. Rome wasn't built in a day, and budgets aren't my strong suit. This time, I'm going to be better.

"A peach sweet tea. Money is in the drawer." She gets back to work, and I grab a few dollars for her drink.

"Cass, you want anything from next door?" I may as well do a group order.

"Oh, iced caramel with cream and sugar, please." She wipes off her hands, then digs some cash out of her pocket to hand it to me.

"You got it," I reply.

"Hey, Stormy, what Kitty said was right. I didn't want to take Laura's appointment. She booked it online. When I called her to cancel, it was harder than I thought it would be to get her to not come." I don't blame Cassidy for a minute, even if she did take Laura on as a client. Money is money. I know that better than anyone else.

"You can't control her. It was bound to happen. Hopefully, we've seen the last of her for a while all the same. I'll be right back." I close the conversation down, feeling lighter after having my own come-to-Jesus meeting with myself. Now maybe the day will go by faster, and I can get home to Griff.

25

GRIFFIN

"Come on, bud, I bet Stormy's almost home for the night." Finn yips in excitement. The boy knows who the woman of the house is by name. After the scene at the salon, I came home, off-loaded my bag, and saw to Finn. Apparently, he didn't forget me after all, even got his lazy self off the couch to greet me at the door. He did his business once I let him outside, leaving the door open while I started a load of laundry, and then it was a shower for me. The first real one after my unintended swim in the ocean. After dealing with the paperwork where Smith is now under investigation, I went back to the place we were staying, changed clothes, grabbed my bag, and hit the fucking road. It felt good to get a couple of hours of sleep in my own bed. What wasn't fun was realizing Finn clearly got a little too comfortable while I was gone. He's going to have a rude awakening coming tonight when Stormy and I are in bed. There's no fucking way I'll have him in bed with us, not when I damn well know I'll be taking Stormy as often as I can, shoulder be damned.

Christ, it's gonna be a pain in the dick for me to be careful. The last thing I need is to re-injure myself and tell Stormy I need surgery. That means my baby girl is going to be riding her daddy's dick tonight. A view I'm going to thoroughly fucking enjoy.

After my nap, I swapped laundry, made a sandwich, some chips, and opened a bottle of beer. My woman keeps the fridge well stocked, a damn blessing. I never did that. I'd stop on my way into work or hit the grocery store on a night I was going to actually be home and pick up what I needed. Now there are fruits, vegetables, the beer I prefer, and whatever else she feels the need to pick up. The difference being now is she cooks dinner early before I have to hit the bar, a reality that's about to change. She'll be getting off work, and I'll be heading out. That's going to suck, big time.

I open the door to the house after taking a walk on the beach with Finn. I'm shirtless and in a pair of board shorts. Finn loves the water, and even though one of my arms is useless, I was still able to toss the frisbee in the water for him to go after. This lasted until he was tired of playing fetch and getting attention from other beach goers, so we started making our way back. A quick rinse in the outdoor shower for both of us to knock off the sand, then drying Finn, and I was ready to see if my woman was home from work.

"Griff," Stormy's greets me, her voice breathless. There she stands in the kitchen, bag on the counter, shoes kicked off, taking her hair out of some kind of clip. I stop just inside the door. Finn goes to Stormy, nudging her hand for attention. She pets his head, eyes never leaving mine. Clearly, we both like what we see with one another, me without a shirt, droplets of water clinging to my skin. My sling is back on after the outdoor shower, but damn if I don't wish it were off right about now.

"Baby girl," I respond, taking another step closer. Stormy's tongue comes out, lapping at her lips, eyes hooded with desire. My baby wants something that only I can give her. Earlier today, her face was full of worry. Now it's filled with desire. We both need one another, which is why I'm walking closer.

"I want you, but I don't want to hurt you." A chuckle escapes me. The only way she'll hurt me is by not touching me.

"You'll have to do all the work. What is it you want, Stormy?" I ask, already knowing what I want. Now I need to hear her say it.

"I want to taste you. I want you in my mouth, Daddy." I'm moving through the living room, grabbing a pillow off the couch along the way. There's a quirk to her eyebrow, wondering why I'd pick it up. She'll figure it out soon enough. Finn moves away, going to his dog bed without me telling him. It seems my boy is on my side today. Gotta love him.

Stormy's eyes don't leave me, not my eyes and definitely not my body. Her head tips to the side at the pillow. She should know I would never have her knees on the cold tile floor. Not when I'm going to fuck that hot mouth of hers.

"Kneel, baby girl, get ready to take your daddy's cock." I drop the pillow to the floor, hand going out to help her get into position. She doesn't hesitate, eyes lowering in desire, nipples pebbling, and I watch as a shudder takes hold of her body. Goddamn, just thinking about sucking my cock is turning her on. My hand is still in hers, and I give her the next task. "Take my dick out." She doesn't need any further encouragement. Stormy's greedy hands attack the strings of my shorts. Velcro gives way, and then my shorts drop to the ground. I step out of them while she waits for my next command.

I'm greeted with a purr when I wrap my hand around my cock. I twist my wrist as I jack my length. Her eyes are on what I'm doing the entire time. She licks her lips, and there goes the last of my restraint.

"You ready for this?" I ask, moving closer. She nods, and I go further. The precum is gathered on the head of my cock. The need to paint her lips with the white pearlescent cum deepens in my chest. "Stay still, let daddy do what he wants, baby girl." I paint her lips. The smooth skin against my cock has my knees locking in place. She gives me a heated look, and I watch her chest rise and fall. This won't last long if I'm not careful. "You wanted to taste me. Lick your lips, and then brace yourself because I'm going to fuck that sweet hot mouth of yours."

"Hmm," she moans when her tongue laps at her lips. Had I thought this through more, I would have had her strip down. As it is now, the second Stormy swallows my cum, I'm going to want a fuck of a lot more than her mouth. I'm going to want her naked, spread on the couch, my head buried between her beautiful-as-fuck thighs.

"Open your mouth for me." She does without question. "Hands on the back of my thighs. Hold on tight. If you need a break, I'll pull back. You might be swallowing my dick, but I won't neglect your need for air or a break." Clearly, she is on the same page because as I take a step closer, my hands going to each side of her head, she wraps her lips around my length. I take a moment to regroup, steadying myself before I lose control. Something I pride myself not to do when it comes to the woman on her knees before me. Today, it might break my will. I slowly slide deeper before pulling out, testing how far I can take it with each pass. Stormy is more than ready. She keeps her tongue soft, tracing the underside of my dick each time.

"Gonna go deeper now," I warn her. One of my hand cups the back of her head. Her eyes water, but she doesn't shake her head no and only becomes more enthusiastic. The tightness in the back of her throat around my tip is an experience like no other. No one but Stormy could ever take me so good. "That's it, baby girl, swallow me, let me feel more," I encourage. My head tips back as a prickling sensation slides up the base of spine, causing my balls to pull tight.

Another moan from her has me pulling my hips back to slide forward again, somehow managing to go deeper. Goddamn, there's no holding back, there's no slowing down, and I hope to fuck she can hold the hell on. I hold her while I fuck her mouth, Stormy taking a piece of my damn soul with the way she matches me.

"Swallow me, baby girl," I groan, my sentence breaking off when she does what I say. Her mouth literally sucks the cum from my body. A ripple takes hold, and I'm not sure if I'll ever recover with each spurt that shoots from me. "Take it all," I say with one last push of my hips, holding her head while I finish coming down her throat. There's no damn way we won't be doing this again. Last time she took me in her mouth, we we're in bed, I was on my back, and she was between my legs. It didn't last long. I couldn't stand not having her cunt wrapped around my dick. Today, though, there was no denying what my woman wanted.

Stormy's hands leave my thighs, and I

slowly pull out of her sweet mouth. "Griff." Her tongue darts out, licking her lips and any remnants of my cum left behind. That's not what has me bending down, though. It's the way she's pressing her thighs together. It's time I take care of her, and I'm going to do that right fucking now.

26

STORMY

One Week Later

"Hey, Barbie, is Griff in his office?" I wave at her while walking toward the bar. Today was slower at the salon, so I went home, let Finn out, and then packed dinner to bring to the bar. I'm hoping it's not one of those nights Griff's on the phone half the time or out on the floor because people are stupid. He's still healing, and I'm making sure he wears the sling even when he says he's fine. Stubborn, stubborn man.

"Hey, Storm. Yeah, he is. It's been a slow one." She winks at me. Usually, she works during the day and not at night. I guess things have changed, or Jeremy is taking time off because she's been her more than usual. I'll have to ask Griff when I make it to his office.

"Thanks." I've got a reusable bag with our dinner. One thing I've come to realize is Griff isn't big on cooking unless it's on a grill. Chicken, steak, pork chops, or burgers, he's got it covered. Sides are not, or anything having to do with the oven. He knows how to cook but prefers it to be outdoors. One day, when I'm out of debt, I'll bring up an idea on building an outdoor kitchen off the back patio. I needed an easy and quick meal for tonight—lemon butter chicken with asparagus cooked in the same pan helped cut down on time. I paired it with rice, and dinner was done in less than forty-five minutes, long enough to change out of my work clothes, feed Finn, and take him for a short walk.

I open the door that leads upstairs, a pep in my step, more than ready to see Griff. I'm at his door in no time, hitting the digits of the keypad he gave me the first night, and I'm opening his door.

"Surprise!" I hold up the bag. Griff had no idea I was coming by tonight. Our schedules are passing at best. Sometimes I get to see him for a quick kiss, others he's already here, and then there's nights like tonight.

"Fuck, you're a sight for sore eyes." He stands up from his seat behind his desk, making quick work until he's to me.

"Everything okay?" There's tension in his eyes, the crinkles showing he's got something going on he hasn't shared.

"Yeah. Had to deal with fucking inventory, and then the report was finished up from the incident. I've been on the phone more than I'd have liked," he says tensely. He told me how everything went down. My mouth was open, and I was gasping because it could have been so much more. A concussion, drowning, my mind went into overdrive with the ideas running through it.

"And what did they have to say?" He drops a kiss to my mouth, hand going to my hip, holding me in place as he takes my lips with his. The man has a wicked way with his mouth, hands, and body. I'm left breathless while he's standing with a smirk on his face.

"Smith is being charged with working under the influence, some kind of upper, and the racing company is looking to press charges. They asked if I wanted to do the same."

"And are you?" I ask. I'd throw the damn

book at this Smith character. He could have killed Griff along with many others.

"Yep, which means if this goes to a trial, I'll have to travel," he states nonchalantly.

"Then I guess I'll be going with you. Now, are you ready for dinner?" I'm hoping our food is still warm. If not, we'll have to microwave it, which isn't a big deal. Everyone knows that re-heating food isn't the same, though.

"More than ready. You want a water or something else?"

"Water. No caffeine, or I'll never sleep. I did that earlier this week, and you remember what happened." It took two rounds of sex to tire me out. Him taking me from behind and the other with me riding him, reverse cowgirl style. A shiver runs through my body remembering just how much Griff was more than up for the occasion. Except I felt bad the next morning when I was getting out of bed and he got up with me.

"You think I'm opposed to that happening again? I've got news for you, baby girl. Anytime you need your daddy, I'm more than ready." And there go my thighs, clenching together, trying to quelch the need he creates.

"Dinner first, then maybe we'll have time for that." I wink and walk toward the couch in his office. The coffee table makes a great impromptu place for eating, and I go about setting out our dinner while Griff grabs our drinks.

The phone rings on his desk. "Goddamn it, the fucking thing won't quit today." I laugh. Griff really isn't a phone person. Calls and texts are short and to the point.

"Hello." His tone is gruff. "What the fuck do you mean they're here and Jack is with them?" Griff pauses. "I'm going to lose my shit on them, Jack included." Another pause. "Yeah yeah, we're fucking coming." He slams down the phone, missing the cradle it's held in, so he slams it again until it finally sits in its resting place.

"Bad news?" I ask. No longer am I unpacking our food. It'll stay warmer in the bag with its insulated layer.

"The fucking worst. Zach, Melissa, and Jack are downstairs. So much for Jack giving me more of a heads-up. Fuckin' dickhead." He runs his hand through his hair, and my thighs clench together at the way his arm muscles flex and his shirt gives way to his stomach. His jeans are sitting low on his hips, and I want nothing more than to trail my tongue until I meet the front of his pants. "Apparently, they want to have some kind of fucking Kumbaya meeting. Jesus, don't they know this is a business, not Grand Central Station?" The look he gives me tell me he liked what he saw. Too bad it can't go further. Stupid people and their stupid timing. I get up from the couch. My feet eat up the distance until I'm in front of him. I place my hand over his heart, trying to calm him down.

"Come on, let's get this show on the road, so maybe it'll finally be closed once and for all." Griff's hand immediately goes to the back of my head, knees dipping so we're on eye level.

"I'm about tired of people trying to hurt my woman, Stormy. This is the last damn time I'm dealing with them. It happens again, I'm busting heads together." I grin. He's in over protective mode, and it only makes me fall in love with him more.

"That's a deal." My lips go to his, kissing him quickly. It seems we're going to face the two people I have no want, will, or desire to, but such is life in a small town. Maybe they'll run away together, forever, and we'll never have to see them again. I mean, it would be bad for Jack, but it would be great for everyone else. Okay, fine, it would be freaking amazing for me at least.

27

GRIFFIN

"You're shitting my dick," I grumble when my eyes clock the idiots standing near the bar. Stormy giggles beside me, my hand on her lower back. Clearly, she's not worried about these damn yahoos. For that I'm fucking grateful. I still see the weight of a few things in her every now and then. Mainly when we talk about money, her trying to pay for more than I think she should, her getting pissy, stomping her foot, and me using my mouth to shut her up.

"Let's get this over with. It can't be that bad, right?" she replies to my verbal annoyance. It seems others are more pissed on her behalf than she is. Barbie's arms are crossed over her

chest, and she's staring daggers at the trio, Jack
included.

"You never know with this bunch." She
shrugs her shoulders. I kiss the top of her head.
I'm attempting to calm my anger with the scent
of her shampoo, coconut and vanilla. It's not
helping, though. The only thing that will is
getting these dumb fucks away from us.

"Hey, Griff, Stormy," Jack greets us first. If
he's trying to break the ice, he could have given
me an advance warning. I'd grab a beer and a
bottle of tequila for Stormy. Alcohol is
inevitably going to be needed.

"Hey, brother. Mel, Zach," I grunt the last
two names. Blood or not, Melissa helped create
this shit storm. I'm not cutting her any fucking
slack. Zach has his own issues, and I'm hopeful
we won't have to see the likes of him around
ever again.

"Hi,"—Stormy pauses—"everyone." Yeah, I
feel the exact same fucking way. This could
have been done out of the public eye, yet we're
not going to get that lucky. Jack moves behind
the bar. Barbie glares at him. Some things
never change.

"Take a seat, baby. You want a drink?" I
ignore the way Mel is trying to get closer and

attempting to say whatever it is she came to say.

"I'm good. Maybe afterwards." She slides onto a barstool. I stay standing, needing to have some semblance of control in case this situation goes from bad to worse.

"Alright," I tell Stormy. My eyes lock on the two idiots in front of me. "Say what you need to say and then leave." I'm not mincing words. These two created a situation that could have been handled if Zach had just stopped the farce of a wedding. I mean seriously, what the fucking fuck? Did he think his shit wouldn't come to light or that Stormy wouldn't divorce his ass if she didn't' find out till after the wedding?

"Stormy, I wanted to tell you. Believe me, I did, but I had no way of coming out," Melissa starts. I grunt, locking eyes with my niece, who is full of shit. Stormy blows out a puff of air. I'm not sure what's going in my woman's mind right now, but it better not be forgiving them so easily. Especially Mel. They've been friends much longer than Zach and Stormy were together.

"Yet still no apology. I think we're done here, Mel." Stormy starts to get up from her seat, clearly done with the conversation, and I'm damn proud.

"That's not all. You deserve to hear it from me instead of others." Mel stops, looks down at her hands, gripping her fingers in a twisting sort of manner. A tell she's nervous. As she fucking should be. She's wreaked havoc on a lot of people, and the dick bag standing next to her is saying not a fucking thing. Well, it shows the lack of balls he has between his legs.

"Then by all means, please get on with it. This whole situation is stupid. Clearly, Zach and I weren't in love. And that's okay, but you two could have fixed this before it got worse. You don't even know the half of what you left me to pick up. I'm not the only adult in this situation, except I am, and if it weren't for Griff rescuing me when he did, I'd have probably come out a lot less unscathed." Damn straight. I squeeze her shoulder in solidarity.

"I know, and I am sorry. We're sorry." Mel points from herself to Zach. He still stays silent. Clearly, Mel wears the pants in this scenario, the entire time, too. I'd be willing to bet she calls the shots in the bedroom. Fucking awful to think about with my own niece, but it says a lot about the man himself. In the bedroom,

Stormy knows I'm in control, even when she's riding my cock or on her knees. I'm not one to give it up. The woman comes alive when I make her stay still while fucking her sweet pussy. "And, well, I didn't want to say it like this or tell Zach." I watch as Melissa looks at Zach like he's hung the moon and stars above. Damn, she's in deep. Zach, on the other hand, doesn't return the favor in the way of looking like he's in love. In fact, the guy looks bored. "I'm pregnant."

You can hear a pin drop. The bar, which had a few others talking, comes to a halt. Even the music is silenced, and I'll bet Barbie has something to do with that.

"Uhh, congratulations," Stormy says, probably at a loss for words. My eyes find Jack's. He's pissed as fucking hell. Obviously, he didn't know anything about this either.

"No fucking way, It's not mine," Zach states vehemently. His face turns red. This is probably the first time he's got an expression on his face that isn't one of boredom.

"What do you mean, it's not yours?" Mel interjects as the door to the bar opens, letting the sunlight in along with someone else to see this shit show come down.

"You gotta be fucking kidding me," I groan, seeing who walks through the door.

"It's not mine," Zach states more firmly.

"What isn't yours?" Laura the cunt Busby has entered the chat. She keeps going, "Oh, you mean the debt Stormy has yet to pay for the ceremony? We know that already." My blood slowly boils. It seems my woman hasn't told me a whole lot about the circumstances left behind from the wedding.

"I've had a vasectomy. The baby isn't mine." Audible gasps come from Zach's mom and Melissa.

"I'm grabbing the vodka. Too bad we don't have popcorn, or I'd settle in," Barbie interjects. My fingers go the bridge of my nose, calming myself down.

"Well, it's not like Zach is going to pay half like we bargained when we planned the wedding. So, excuse the fuck out of me if I'm trying to make sure I can survive in order to pay something off that I didn't want in the damn first place." Stormy hops down from her seat, starting to get closer to Zach and his mom. I hold her back even if my hand is itching to come down on her ass.

"What do you mean, you had a vasectomy? Why does that even matter?" Laura says, ignoring Stormy. I sure as fuck haven't. We'll be getting back to that subject as soon as these fucks get out of here.

"How could you have a vasectomy without telling me? You said you wanted kids, that we'd have a future," Mel exclaims.

"I said I wanted kids. I didn't say when. I'd have gotten a reversal, but now that's out, and so am I." He turns on his heel to leave. Melissa is reaching for his arm, but he's shaking her off with each step he takes. Mel wants his attention so bad she keeps after him.

"We're talking about this. You kept something from me that I could have helped you with." I bend down to whisper into Stormy's ear.

"No, no way. You've helped me in more ways than those assholes ever have. I'm going to pay it off. Everything else, the deposits handled. I'll pay those back to my mom, and I'll deal with the ceremony."

"Yes, you will, little girl. I'm not responsible for your debt," Laura interrupts.

"Get fucked, lady." I look directly at Laura. Her son is creating more damn drama, and she's worried about a debt Stormy is going to attempt to handle on her own. Absolutely the fuck not.

"You can't talk to me like that." My arm is still wrapped around Stormy's chest, holding her in place. Anger is vibrating off her waves. Now I'm done, completely fucking done.

"Listen the fuck up, right the fuck now!" I get everyone's attention. Barbie smirks. She knows when I've met my threshold and is already reaching for the bat we keep behind the bar. "Get the fuck out of my bar now. Everyone fucking out." I point at Laura. "Including you. Your fucking son will pay half, or he'll deal with me. As for you, go figure out why your son decided to have an affair with my niece while being engaged."

That shuts her up. Barbie grabs Jack's hand. The other patrons are already leaving. A good thing it's mainly the usual bar goers, or I'd be fucked. It's also a Tuesday evening, so it's slow as hell.

"We're not done here," Laura stammers.

"Out, get the hell out." I walk closer, keeping Stormy in front of me the entire time. No way am I letting her go right now. I'm liable to do something to the cunt in front of us, and then I'd be in jail. Never once have I wanted to hit a woman in my life. Laura has made me re-think it one too many times.

"You heard the man. I'm locking up. The

bar is closed for the night." Barbie comes around the bar, bat in her hand, and everyone scatters like cockroaches. I don't move a muscle until the last person leaves, waiting for Barbie to lock the wood door, and when she does, I'll take this a lot fucking further. I'm going to let Stormy know exactly the man I am. Taking care of her is as easy as breathing, and it's time she realizes that. Tonight.

28

STORMY

"Strip, baby girl, now." Griff lets go of me, moving until he's standing in front of me, hands on his hips and a look in his eyes I can't determine.

"Griff, I was going to tell you. Promise. I was trying to figure out how to open my books or ask for a job here at the bar." My words don't help the situation, not at all. Griff walks me toward me, one step forward from him is one step backward for myself. He doesn't stop until my back meets the bar. His hand goes to my shirt. It appears if I'm not going to strip, he is going to do it for me.

"I don't like that at all. You working more means less time for us. You give me a lot, baby girl. Let me help you." My arms rise without hesitation, leaving me in my bra and skirt. A look that clearly Griff likes with the way he's eyeing me up and down.

"Not enough, not nearly enough." I feel like there are times I'm lacking bringing anything to the table, money especially.

"You give me a lot, and not in the financial aspect, because I give zero fucks about that. It's the soft touches, the cooked dinners, the way you love Finn like he's your own dog, and Stormy,"—his hand cups my cheek, thumb sliding over my lower lip as he continues— "the way you say *daddy*. Fuck, it makes me come undone. You give me everything."

"No, I don't give you enough, but that's how I feel. It's not a reflection of you." The words are bitter to admit even to my own ears.

"Then it's time for me to show you just how much you give me. Clearly, words aren't enough." His hands grip my hips, lifting me up. A sense of déjà vu from the first time we were together in his bar hits me. "Up on the bar, and spread your legs while I eat your pussy," he commands, fire in is tone. I know it's killing him not to pick me up and do what he wants, but his shoulder needs to recover first. I unfasten the buttons of my jean skirt that are in a row down the middle, leaving me with my bra, panties, and shoes. I'm not taking my shoes off. No offense to Griff's bar, but I know what people leave behind on the floors. As far as the bar top, it's constantly sanitized.

"Griff," I groan when I see him undo the button to his jeans. The hiss of his zipper is silent given the music is still playing in the background. What I don't miss is his hard cock coming into view, long and thick. The tips of my fingers barely meet when I wrap them around him.

"Baby girl, you're getting my mouth, but in order to do that, I need you on the bar." It seems Griff is losing his patience, and I, for one, do not want to test him any longer. My hands go to the bar, using the ledge and my upper body until my ass lands on the wood counter. It's cool to the touch. A hiss leaves my lips. "Been wanting you like this. Thought about it for a while now. Maybe you'll realize you give me everything." He pulls a barstool in front of where I'm sitting, hands going to the inside of my thighs. I obviously didn't have them spread wide enough.

"I don't know. It seems you may have to show me at least a few times." He can't really blame me, can he? The man has a way with working me over in the best possible way.

"Every single day, I'll prove it to you, if that's what it takes. Take your bra off," he replies with another demand. My hand moves behind my back. The other stays on the bar top, holding myself up. "Good girl," I'm praised when my bra drops down with a flick of the clasp. Griff's hands slide up my thighs further, the tips of his fingers getting dangerously close to the edge of my panties only to pull away again.

"Please," I beg when his head lowers, and he blows a breath of air along my center. The lace does nothing to shield the coolness that's heating my fevered flesh.

"Please, what, baby girl?" His thumb hooks on the edge of the fabric, ripping it to the side and baring my pussy to his watchful eyes.

"Please, Daddy." That's all it takes. Griff's head dips further, and I watch as he takes one long lick from the bottom to the top. His tongue swirls, lips wrapping around my clit and sucking on it. I lose my hold, eyes closing and hands giving way until I'm flat on my back. All the while, Griff keeps working my pussy. The man is obsessed. The groans he lets lose vibrate against my core, and it's setting my world on fire. I'm trying to stay still even with the need to put my hand on the back of his head and flex my hips upward. I know better, though. Griff would stop. I'd lose the orgasm I'm barreling toward. He'd make me settle down, and only then would he work me up again.

"Oh God." I need something. "More, please more," I plead. Keeping my hands flat on the bar is killing me. There's no purchase, nothing to squeeze or to clench my fingers around. I'm left feeling an emotional upheaval as my orgasm bubbles to the surface. Griff's tongue slides inside my center, working it like he would with his cock, thumb going to my clit, rubbing it up, down, then side to side. My eyes clench shut, sweat coats my body, and I'm soaring, flying sky high with an intensity that only Griff can give me. It's like an out-of-body experience, a floating sensation, and through it all, he doesn't leave his place between my thighs. His pace slows down, licking and soothing me through the remnants of my orgasm until I'm no longer able to withstand any more. "Too much," I murmur.

"You better prepare because you're about to ride my cock next, baby girl." He lifts his head, lips and chin slick with my wetness, but he doesn't seem to care. I use my hands to lift my body up, more than ready to feel his hard length inside of me.

"You're trying to kill me. I once again can't feel my legs." I'm greeted with a grin. His hands slide to my waist, pulling me until I'm closer to the edge of the bar. It takes all my might to maintain my balance while not giving Griff my weight with his shoulder in a sling.

"Are you saying you don't want my cock?" He arches a brow. I shake my head in a vehement no. "That's what I thought. I'll help you down. Grip my good shoulder." He guides me down, his length already out and ready, the head of his cock weeping with precum. I almost wish we had more room. I'd dip my head and take it with my tongue.

"Can I help?" I ask Griff, my hand wanting to wrap around his dick to guide inside me while I continue lowering myself.

"Yeah, baby girl, wrap your hand around daddy's cock until the tip is inside, then hands to yourself." His dominant side is always at the surface, but when it's the two of us like this, there's no holding himself back. My hand wraps around his smooth velvet length. Feeling it flex causes me to squeeze it once. "Fucking Christ," he groans. My knees meet the leather of the barstool, old fashioned style where they have a back and a seat big enough to allow us the room to be in our current state.

"Daddy." I do more than what he stated, coating his tip with my wetness. A low groan escapes.

"Hands off. Wrap them around my shoulder and hold the fuck on. You know what I like, baby girl," he reiterates. His hands hold my hips, and I barely have enough time until he's slamming me down and fucking his cock inside of me. All I can do is hold on and enjoy every moment with Griff taking me exactly how we like it.

29

STORMY

"Hey, Kitty, I'm out of here." It's been a few days since the night at the bar. After Griff had his way with me, we went home, where we talked and talked. Griff wasn't having me working more, and honestly, he was right. Another swallow of my pride was admitting that I needed help. I put the ceremony on my credit card, paid off what I could with what was in my savings account, and Griff said he'd handle the rest. Mom wouldn't let me give her the deposits back, which meant I had more to pay on my credit card. That was a fight for another day. My will to deal with much more was lackluster at best.

"Have a good rest of your day. See you tomorrow, honey." I grab my purse from my chair after a successful day. My books are open to a few new clients, not only for the money either. Which Griff said I don't need, but tell that to my independence. It worked out in the end, though. I lost a few clients, Melissa being one of them. It goes without saying I fired her from my book. Then another moved in with her family a few hours north, and another went back to college for the fall semester. That left me with room for three plus a few more while keeping my same hours. The plan to work weekends while Griff is away is now obviously out the window.

"You do the same." I walk out the door, ready to get home before Griff has to leave for work. Maybe we'll have enough time to eat dinner together, or he could stay home. I'm in the middle of devising a plan, like walking in the house, taking off all my clothes, and finding him. Another idea is putting the outside shower to use, changing into one of my bikinis, then finding Griff on the beach with Finn. I'd lure him into the water, tease him for as much as he'd allow before darting back up to the house. Of course, I couldn't strip like I could inside the house. Griff would lose his ever-loving mind, and I'm not interested in giving the beach goers or our neighbors a peep show.

"Stormy," I hear my name, but no one would be trying to get ahold of me. Kitty had a client, Mom has a date tonight, and Aunt Cat is out of town doing a solo vacation in the mountains. Now that things have settled down, they're finally doing their own thing. "Stormy, wait, please!" Okay, not hearing things. I'd recognize that voice anywhere.

I don't want to stop walking. I'd much rather keep going. My car is in sight, and I'm almost scot-free. "Hold on just a minute, Stormy, please." I close my eyes, stopping my stride, refusing to turn around. Melissa is going to have to realize not everything will go her way.

"Stormy, I know I'm the last person you want to see." Only when she's in front of me do I give her the attention she's after. Griff's borrowed sunglasses are doing wonders right about now; the mirrored lenses block my eyes. My eyes show my resting bitch face far too easily, and these are helping Mel see that I'm unbothered by her presence. At least I'm perceived that way. She doesn't need to know that my stomach drops and the need to run away is flowing through my nervous system.

"Melissa, I don't think we have anything left to say to one another." I remain calm. The last thing we need is to have this out in the public, which sadly means I need to bring her to my car. "That being said, I'd rather the whole town not hear our conversation, or rumors are going to be spread yet again."

"You're right. I tried calling and texting you, but they didn't go through," she admits.

"Aunt Cat had a field day with my phone. You and about nine other people are blocked. It's staying that way." I start walking. Melissa falls into step beside me. It wasn't long ago this would be our Sunday morning routine after having brunch and one too many mimosas or Bloody Mary's. I think that's what I miss the most—not Zach, but my best friend. The person who knows me through and through.

"I figured as much. Can we go somewhere and talk?"

"I'm walking us in the direction of a bench around the corner. I'm not having this discussion where every Tom, Dick, and Harry can report back to the town gossip. Been there, done that, paying the debt off for it, too." My sarcastic side has come out to play.

"I deserved that," Mel says as we turn the corner. I breathe a sigh of relief. There's no one else around.

"Give me a minute. I need to text Griff to let him know I'll be late getting home." Melissa starts to smile at me. I shake my head no. She doesn't deserve to know what's going on in my relationship with Griff. I pull my phone out of my back pocket. Today, I dressed down. The heat was at an all-time high, and there was no way pants were going to be an option. A pair of cut-off jean shorts, a white tank top, and sandals were an easy decision. I'm so glad Kitty doesn't have a dress code, or I'd have quit already.

> Me: Hey, going to be late getting home. Melissa wants to talk. If I don't text again in thirty minutes, rescue me ;)

I'm about to put my phone in my back pocket when it vibrates. Griff is already responding.

> Griff: Make it fifteen, and the cavalry will head your way.

> Me: So, you and Finn?

Griff: Hell fucking yes.

His favorite word starts with *f* and ends with a *k, s,* or *ing.* Any variable will do, really. I sit down on the picnic bench across from Melissa and put my forearms on the table, hands hugging each elbow.

"I'm sorry. I should have said that first. I was only thinking of myself, I see that now. I was jealous of what you had, and I wanted something that wasn't mine." I'm listening to Melissa, but all I'm hearing is me, myself, and I. Still, I let her keep going. "I'm not even pregnant. Zach didn't want me. He wanted the thrill of the chase. Once he had me and you knew about us being together, the fun was over. I'm stupid and knew I was losing him and threw out I was pregnant to try and make him stay."

I take a deep breath. My once best friend is insecure, and that really sucks. Because not once did I see this side of her during out entire friendship.

"It hurts, and it sucks. You let a man get between our friendship and self-sabotaged yourself in the process. You created a rift that was unnecessary in doing so. It also made me re-evaluate life. Zach and I were never in love, obviously for him. As for myself, I found

someone who truly makes time for me and I
can see myself with forever." Melissa has black
tears trailing down her cheeks, her mascara
making it worse. "So, I guess I'm thankful in
that sense. It helped me in a way, even with my
name being raked through the coals. I came
out better for it." I end my sentence, feeling a
peace inside me I wasn't aware I needed.
Another door closing for another one to open.
It's called closure, and I'm glad I have it.

"I really am sorry, Stormy. My words or
actions aren't enough, I know that. Maybe one
day, we can be friends again." I shake my head.
My tongue goes to the roof of my mouth,
holding back a smart-aleck remark. Melissa
must get that I'm not about that, not one single
bit. It also gives me a moment to gather my
thoughts. I'm no longer mad or angry, so there's
no reason to wish ill will against her. Karma
sounds amazing and all that, but asking for
karma against someone else, asking to receive
it back?

"Sometimes, Mel, sometimes friendships
can't be salvaged. Unfortunately, there's too
much of a history with us and a lot of trauma
and damage as well. I'll remain cordial. Griff
and Jack deserve that much. I may not like that
we're linking in such a way, especially with the

way things are progressing with Griff, but I'll do it for him." And I will. Griff would never make me either; he's selfless like that.

"I understand. Thank you for talking with me. I'll, uh, see you around." She stands up first to leave.

"See you around," I respond, staying in my seat and watching her leave. Overall, today was another great day, and it's about to get a lot better. I stand up, take my phone out again, and shoot Griff a text.

> Me: Heading home. See you soon.

Griff must have been on pins and needles waiting for my text or a call because he's already responding. The bubble appears, and then so does his message.

> Griff: We're here waiting for you. Everything go okay?

> Me: Yeah, it did, actually. I'll tell you about it when I get home.

> Griff: Drive safe.

> Me: Always.

I keep my phone in my hand, pull my keys

out of my pocket, and head to my car. I've got a man and our dog waiting for me at home, and I can't wait to have Griff's arms wrapped around me. That's the one thing that will make this day even better.

30

GRIFFIN

I'm waiting in the kitchen, wondering how Stormy is dealing. Will she come home in tears, pissed at the world, or will she pretend to be alright until she isn't? One thing I know for sure, we're going to talk it out, get the hard shit out of the way and focus on the good.

"I hear ya, boy. She'll be here in in a couple of minutes." I don't tell him we'll be on the beach soon enough. He'd go crazy, bark, wiggle his ass while his grinch-like toes dance on the tile. "You need an appointment with the groomers." Finn groans, his least favorite part of being a dog. The boy has it made. He doesn't even leave the house. A van pulls up in the driveway, she grooms him, and within an hour, he's back to either hitting the beach or sleeping on the couch.

The whir of the garage door is heard in the quiet house. I chose to turn the TV off after her text talking about meeting with Mel. I was half tempted to call Jack. Maybe he could put a damn leash on that daughter of his. I head to the fridge, grab a bottle of beer for myself, open the freezer, and get the bottle of tequila Stormy prefers. Even if she doesn't need a drink to help decompress, tonight is one to celebrate. A few more ingredients, a flavored seltzer water, a lime, some ice cubes later, and then I get to work on her drink. Stormy doesn't mind drinking tequila on the rocks. That's not happening today. She'll be completely coherent when I tell her how much she means to me.

"Hey, Finn." I look to the side while squeezing the rest of the lime before dropping it into her class with the rest of the ingredients. Stormy is on her knees, bag dropped to the side, giving the big lug a hug while she dodges his tongue from licking her face. I'd tell him to relax, but Stormy would counteract my demand and say he's fine. I let them have their time together. "Were you a good boy today?"

"If you mean coming home to a pile of fur,

legs up, dog flat on his back, tail wagging, and in our bed good, then yeah, he had a great day." Before Stormy, my bedroom door would stay shut during the day to keep him off the bed. When I was gone for those few days, Stormy changed a lot, including my way of thinking. Finn is now king of the house more than ever. She doesn't seem to care that we now have two vacuums going in the middle of the day to help with the dog hair. She also doesn't mind that our bed needs to be lint rolled or a blanket put over the comforter and pillows anytime we leave. I told her to shut the bedroom door one time, and she gave me an earful. I laughed and conceded in order not to make a big deal out of something she enjoys.

"Still salty about that, are we?" I take a step back from the counter, the neck of the beer wrapped in my knuckles, and her glass in my hand.

"It creates more work for you, so yeah, I am." Once I'm in front of her, I offer my free hand to help her up. The sling is as needed these days. The damn thing is a nuisance. One that Stormy made sure I wore non-stop until the doctor cleared me yesterday, a week earlier than I thought he would.

"You help me, so it's not so bad. Is this for

me?" she asks, standing up. My look must say it all. Tequila is not my preference. If I'm drinking liquor, it's going to be bourbon. Otherwise, I stick to beer. "Hmmm, this is so good." She takes a sip, her tongue licking around the edge of the class. The Tajin along the rim is her favorite part after the tequila.

"Kiss, baby girl." My head dips as hers comes up, my tongue gaining entrance immediately. There's no pretense. Stormy knows what I like, and I give her what she likes right back. My hand guides hers until she's pressing her palm against my chest, then I'm deepening the kiss. Her tongue chases mine, and a groan rumbles from the back of my throat.

"Griff," she breathes as my mouth moves from hers, tipping her head back since my hand navigated toward her hair while we were kissing.

"Damn, Stormy, you go to my head faster than a shot of bourbon." It's a wonder neither of us spilled our drink on one another.

"The feeling is mutual." I press a kiss against her one last time.

"Go change. We'll meet you on the beach. I promised Finn we'd take him to the beach when you got home." Stormy's face turns soft, liking that we waited on her when usually, I'd have it done before she's off work.

"I won't be but a minute!" She takes another sip of her drink, hands the glass back to me, and runs to the bedroom. Her hands are already at the tight tank top she's wearing, pulling it over her head and going for the clasp behind her back. Jesus Christ, just like that, I'm rock fucking hard, rethinking meeting her at the beach. I'd do it, too, follow her into the room, pin her to the mattress, and fuck my cock into her sweet pussy while I tell her the words I'm more than ready to say.

"Come on, boy, before you miss out on your evening routine." I put both of our drinks on the counter, pull my shirt off, and toss it on a barstool. My eyes catch on the built-in book-case. Stormy asked for help to put her feather collection up on a higher shelf. I was still in a sling, and she wouldn't let me grab the ladder. Instead, she told me to hold her steady. She climbed on top of it by stepping on the cabinets beneath. My hand creeped up the back of her thigh, grabbed a handful of her ass after she put the red brick with drilled holes in it for each feather. I was more than prepared for her to knock my hand away, and when she needed help down, it was me who stopped her once she was on her ass, thighs spread, and nothing on besides my shirt. A quick pull on the string to my pajama pants had my cock at the ready, and since Stormy was slick with wetness, I took advantage. Her arms wrapped around my shoulders, and I used my good arm to loop the back of her knee over my forearm and fucked her while she stayed exactly as I placed her.

Everywhere I look, there are reminders of Stormy and myself together, and after this evening, there are going to be a fuck of a lot more.

31

STORMY

I walk out the back door, my steps hurrying, feeling like I'm missing out on the best time of the day. The sun is slowly setting, and the beach is calm and quiet in the sense that there aren't a lot of people now. My feet leave the grass after I open the gate and hit the sand, and my eyes lock on Griff. His back is to me, and I watch as he throws the ball for Finn to run off and catch, only to repeat the process again and again until one of us is tired. Most of the time, it's me. Finn gives me the out, goes to Griff, then is finally worn out. I soak in the moment, but not for too long. If I wait too much longer, a certain man will have no problem cutting it short at the beach in order to bring me down with him.

Griff turns around, giving me a devastating smile, one that he doesn't give just anybody. He's got a pair of board shorts on, hitting him a little lower than mid-thigh, and no shirt. I guess I was right to put on my bikini, especially with the way he's drinking my body up. My pace quickens, ready to be near him. It's then I notice the small table he brought down. Usually, we only set it up if we're using the chairs. Today, it holds our drinks, and I love the thoughtfulness in knowing what I'd need before I knew it.

"Hi." My chest fills with air before I let it out once I'm close enough for him to hear me over the ocean kissing the shoreline. It doesn't stop, no matter how many times the waves are sent away.

"Hey, baby, you good?" His hand comes out, capturing the loose hair slipping out of my ponytail and tucking it behind my ear.

"I'm good. Great, really. Life is settling down. Melissa gave me some closure I needed even though I probably could have been fine without it. I came home to you for the night, unless you're going to the bar tonight?" I probably shouldn't have assumed Griff was staying home tonight. If I had taken the chance to look around the kitchen, I'd have gotten a better idea. I didn't, but the drinks he made had me thinking differently. Griff doesn't usually drink on a night he heads to work.

"Good, I'm glad, and you've got me for the entire night. Jeremy is back in town. He and Barbie are managing the shifts. We're going to move Nav up to bartending if he'd like the position. It's easier to find barbacks than it is a bartender, and the kid deserves a raise." I roll my eyes. Nav is older than me by a few years. Griff is showing his age with that statement.

"I'm a very lucky woman, then, and does that mean you'll be home at night more?" I'm pressing for answers, but if things go the way they should, it won't take me long to get my savings account back to where it was. Griff being Griff refuses to let me help with the household bills. The house is paid off; that leaves the utilities and groceries. Thankfully, since I cook more than he does, I can contribute with food, the one task he hates, shopping of any kind and definitely cooking indoors.

"I fucking hate leaving when you're coming home. I hate that you're crawling out of bed when I just got you wrapped around my body. Something's gotta change, baby girl." His arm wraps around my shoulder, pulling me into his body when Finn comes running back. A wet and slobbery ball is in his mouth, ready to be thrown. I wrinkle my nose. I'm not wearing shorts to wipe my hands off on. Griff can have fun with that.

"Really?" I can't manage the excitement in my voice.

"Yeah, we both need it. I'm not getting any younger, and I need my rest to keep up with you." What a crock of shit. It's entirely the other way around. The man is a freaking powerhouse. One round somehow always leads to another.

"Are you're complaining?" I tease.

"Not on your life, baby girl." He throws the ball for Finn, since he's prancing back and forth, starting to talk in order to get his way.

"I have some news of my own. I lost three clients this month. I was thinking about opening my books for new ones." The growl Griff gives off has me cover his mouth yet again. "If you're done, I'll continue." I laugh at his nod. It's killing him not to make a comment. "But with the stipulation of no longer working weekends." It's a bold move that could possibly backfire on me. I want lazy weekends with Griff, sitting on the back deck watching Finn play while we drink a cup of coffee. Griff scoots our chairs closer, moving my legs until they're on top of his, and runs his fingers along my skin, causing goose bumps to appear.

"Fuck yeah, I like that, Stormy, a whole hell of a lot." His head dips, and his lips graze mine. I'm yearning for more except he pulls away too soon. Now it's me annoyed and him smirking. "Come on, sit with me, and I'll give you more of what we both want." Griff takes my hand, leading me until we're closer to the table. There I see a blanket spread out. He's got everything under control, it seems.

"You had this all planned out, didn't you?" I ask once he's setting down, hand up in the air for mine, his ass on the blanket, feet planted, and legs spread.

"Yep, since this morning." He pats the place between his thighs, and I make sure not to bring more sand on the blanket than necessary while planting myself where he wants me.

"And what all do you have planned?" I ask. He hands me my drink, then grabs his for himself. His other hand goes to my lower stomach.

"Lean back, baby girl. Enjoy the view." He doesn't realize while the view may be pretty, there's nothing better than being with him.

Finn nudges the ball with his nose, the waves carry it, and he runs after it a few more times. I take another sip of my drink, chuckling when Finn loses interest in his ball and chases after a few birds. Griff's fingers graze my lower abdomen, causing me to inhale deeply, and I swear his pinky slides beneath my bottoms before I can catch sight of it. "You finished with your drink?" he asks, placing his bottle on the table.

"I am, thank you." I tip my head back, maneuvering myself so I can see more of his handsome face. "Those two words don't convey nearly enough how grateful and thankful I am to have you in my life. Everything you've done and continue to do."

"Shut up, Stormy. You've thanked me enough, and I'll be damned if you say those three words first. Ain't no fucking way. This time, I'm interrupting you, and keep your hands where I can see them." He smirks, taking my hand not wrapped around his leg, holding it tightly, completely unknowingly, too. "I don't give a shit what others think. They could have thought I left that sham of a wedding with you on my arm, your dress in shambles, and thinking we had the wildest sex ever. I wouldn't have cared as long as you weren't in a vulnerable situation. That being said, gossipers are going to gossip. Let them. My love for you runs through my veins deep into my heart. You're my world. I love you, Stormy." Griff is right. People will say this is too soon, that I'm jumping from one relationship to the next. Hell, they probably already did when I moved in with him. I don't care. Not at all. They're not a quarter of what Griff is. He's got more love in his pinky finger than they have in their heart.

"I love you, Griff. I don't care what others think or say. As long as you're by my side, that's all I care about." One minute I'm sitting between Griff's lap, the next I'm flat on my back, his arms are caging me in, and his mouth is descending on mine.

"Fucking right. Soon, you'll have my ring on your finger, my baby in your belly, and maybe a few more."

"Are you telling me this or asking, because four babies is two too many. Geesh, I still have a salon to own. That's going to be kind of hard with a houseful of kids." Griff doesn't miss a beat. His nose slides along mine, and he lowers his lips until they are hovering above mine.

"You can do anything with me by your

side." There he goes again, baring it all to me,
heart and soul.

"Kiss me," I beg, unable to take it much
longer. The need to burst into tears out of
sheer happiness is on the edge.

"Bossing me around again. We'll see where
that lands you. Grab the blanket, baby girl.
Daddy needs you." His arm snakes beneath my
back, my legs locking around his hips. I grab
the blanket as Griff stands up with me in his
arms. "Fuck it. I'll come back for the table."
One hand grabs our drinks in one swift movement, the other going to my ass.

"Daddy," I whimper into his ear with each
step he takes, feeling his hard cock slide
against my center. Griff takes it a notch further,
hand delving beneath my bathing suit
bottoms. The tips of his fingers press into the
cheeks of my ass, moving lower until he's
teasing my pussy.

"Finn, let's go, boy!" He whistles. "Two
more minutes. Can you hold for me that long,
Stormy?" There's a tightness in his tone, and
I'm wondering who needs whom more.

"Yes, but hurry." I drop my hips, unable to
stand the sensation rolling through my body.

"I'm hurrying, baby girl. Gonna take you in
the outdoor shower first then work our way

through the house. That way, when you're finally ready to have my baby in your belly, all our practice will make it perfect." He isn't playing fair. The more he talks about children, the more I'm tempted to go to my doctor and get the implant taken out of my arm.

"Promise?"

"With all my heart." His mouth attaches to mine, my arms tighten their hold, and I'm lost in Griff Hawkins, forever.

EPILOGUE

GRIFFIN

Two Years Later

"Come on, Stormy, you're going to be late to your own grand opening," I tell my wife while holding the gate open for her at the edge of the yard. Today is the day she's finally opening the salon. Kitty was finally ready to hang up her apron, and Stormy was more than ready. I'd have bought it for her, or a place of her own, if she'd let me. Damn independence streak. We went round and round. Finally, I told her she doesn't have to do it alone, and she replied she knew that. I dropped the subject, knowing the minute we were married, I could gift her the damn place, and there wasn't fuck all she could do about it.

"I'm coming, I'm coming. This child of yours is making it difficult to sleep, let alone walk." Stormy was up three times last night having to pee. I'd wake up right along with her, rub her back until she fell back asleep only to repeat the same process two more times. She's grumbling now, but I see the way her hand rubs her belly and the boy she's carrying inside it.

"He's mine and not yours today? He must be giving you a run for your money." The long burnt-orange dress she's wearing shows of her swollen belly. It wasn't long after we got married that Stormy sat me down and said it was time for her to make an appointment. An appointment I went with her to watch as the doctor took out her birth control. It took all I had not to come unglued watching as they numbed Stormy beneath her arm, made a small incision, and remove the implant. Never fucking again was she doing that. My wife was ready to start a family. Not even a minute later, I had us both stripped naked and took her against the first available surface.

"I could barely bend over." She has a new feather in her hand, one to add to her collection. The addition of them is more prevalent now than when I met her; the brick she created before moving in is now mostly full. I swept up one the day I told her I loved her, giving it to her later in the evening. Another one when I asked her to marry me. And the last one before today was when we found out she was pregnant.

"You got the feather, though," I respond. My hand moving to cup her stomach, and I dip low to kiss my wife. There's something about watching her waddle, seeing the glow in her face, and knowing she's nurturing our child with her ever-changing body.

"I got the feather. We keep adding so many amazing milestones, I'm going to need another display." She rubs her fingers together, making the feather swirl. There's no way we'll be on time now. Stormy will need to wash the feather and undoubtedly go to the bathroom again, whether it's due to our boy or to make sure her hair is in order.

"I'll work on that tomorrow. Now, hand over the feather. I'll wash it, you go do what needs to be done before we're any later than we already are." Finn comes up behind me, barking, trying to get our attention. Stormy thought about bringing him with us today, but after thinking it through, she figured it'd be too boring for the lazy lug.

"Fine. I'm not sure why I'm feeling nervous. Everything's done, the place was set up, and the caterer is meeting us there. You made sure the alcohol would be ready, right?" When Stormy bought the salon from Kitty, she did a massive overhaul. While Kitty was more into a country style theme, Stormy brought her own style to the table. Unfortunately, it meant a whole lot of blood, sweat, and tears. The later from her and others from me. No fucking way was I letting her climb a step stool to paint. Even if she wasn't pregnant, I wouldn't have allowed it. Now that she is, my protective side is a lot worse. And it's made us have a few arguments over the last few months.

"Barbie is there now. She said the place looks great. There's wine and beer in the coolers, and Nav is on his way to play bartender." Stormy had an idea where we'd serve mixed drinks. I nixed that idea. No way would she want to pull the permits in order to deal with that headache. Wine and beer, you don't need one, and it's less of a headache for her, along with not having to worry about people getting shit-faced drunk.

"You're a lifesaver. In case I haven't thanked

you lately, thank you." Her hand touches my cheek, pulling me down as she reaches for my mouth.

"Quit thanking me, woman. I'm here. Always," I tell her before taking her mouth with mine, unable to make this short and sweet. Fuck it, we'll be late for all I care. Her mouth is too sweet, her moans too tempting, and knowing that she gives in to me so easily, it's no wonder I'm always buried inside my wife.

"Griff," she moans, allowing me access to lick my way inside, deepening our kiss. Anytime I'm with Stormy, I forget everything; it falls to the wayside. The noise in my head about the bar, her salon, her impending due date in the next two weeks, it all quiets down.

"We're coming back to that, but first, you gotta appear at the salon. At least for an hour, then I'll take you to the back room and make good on my promise." Her hands clench my shirt, silently begging for more. Damn, we seriously should have rethought opening the salon until after Heath was born. As it is now, if we don't show up, her mom and aunt will come running toward the house thinking she's in labor. They're not above using the keypad and gaining entry, a code my wife keeps giving

them even though I change it monthly. Stormy
just gives them the code again, just in case, or
some measly excuse.

"Promise?" As if she even needs to ask.

"That's a guaran-fuckin-tee, baby girl."
She's breathless, I'm rock hard, and now we
really need to get going. "Come on, let's get this
show on the road." I move over so she can walk
in front of me. It gives me the perfect opportu-
nity to smack her ass, too. The glare she throws
over her shoulder does nothing except make
me harder.

"I am, I am. Yeesh." Not yet, she isn't, but
soon, she'll be coming on my fingers, mouth,
and then my cock.

The end of BARING IT ALL

**I hope you enjoyed Griff and Stormy's story
and will consider leaving a review. The next
book, His For The Taking is coming soon and
you can find their prologue below.**

Want more Men in Charge? His For The
Taking A Single Dad Small Town Romance is
coming October 15th!

Amazon

Prologue
Jameson

One Week Earlier

"Come on Josephine, let's play while we
wait for momma to get here," I tell my nearly
two-year-old daughter. Her mom and I aren't
together, each of us were scratching an itch, a
busted condom, and now here's Josephine.
Those that tell you that you can't feel when a
rubber breaks is a dumb ass liar. I pulled out, it
wasn't in enough time. She knew the moment
it happened. A few weeks later when Emma
called me, I knew what it was about. There was
no doubt in my mind that Josephine was mine.
Emma is a lot of things, a liar isn't one of them.
We knew the two of us were like oil and vine-
gar. One night and a handful of talks later once

the doctor's appointments were out of the way, we set up a game plan. There wasn't a chance in hell we wouldn't be toxic to one another, friendship is way better than two people vehemently hating one another for the rest of Josephine's life.

Emma and I are type A personalities, both competitive, both hardworking in our respective careers, and both control freaks We knew it'd be a recipe for disaster. I went with her to every appointment, and anytime a new milestone was hit Emma would call me. It didn't matter if the baby kicked, if she had weird cravings, or if the doctor said her blood sugar wasn't in the right parameters. We kept an open line of communication and still do.

"Ma-ma coming?" Josephine's baby blues light up her entire face. The perfect combination of Emma and myself. Our girl has soft blonde hair like I had as a child that turned darker, my blue eyes. Her mouth, eyes, and lips, well those are all Emma's. Today she's decked out in a white frilly top, white and pink belle bottom style jeans. A gift from my brother and his wife the last time they stopped by, it's now a repeat outfit for Josephine and far be it from me to fight with her over clothes. Oh no, we deal with that enough when it comes to her hair. I'm a guy, I get that I'm not the best. I've tried the trick of using the hairbrush to get the bumps out of her ponytail, making sure it's wet, and have even attempted the vacuum cleaner trick to get it all secure back. It's never what Josephine wants and try as I might, Emma does it better. So, when she's with me it's a sloppy whatever I can manage to do. I've got big fucking hands and big fucking fingers.

"She'll be here in a few minutes," I look down at my watch, seeing the time for Emma to arrive is later than usual. She's usually prompt or will call to give me a heads up unless a meeting kept her later than normal and she can't pull her phone out. A cooperate lawyer forty minutes on the outskirts of town means she's in the thick of it. Our schedule of sharing Josephine works. We trade off four days one week, three days the next, and if we need a breather or something comes up, we work around it. While we're at work my parents help with Josephine for the most part though we're supposed to be interviewing schools next week. I'm not sold on the idea, Josephine is barely two and I hate the thought of her being around strangers when my parents love having her during the day a few days a week. So far that's been our biggest hurdle, I've asked Emma to reconsider it, and so far it's gone unanswered.

"How about if we look inside the fridge for dad. I've gotta eat dinner and snacks ain't cuttin' it," the coffee table has leftover snack remnants, my girl is a grazer, and I'm one hundred percent Josephine's snack bitch.

"Da-da, up!" Josephine holds her arms up in the air once I'm standing from the floor. The living room is a mess of toys, blankets, and pillows from our afternoon after she woke up from her nap.

"I hear you, princess," I bend down to pick her up, Josephine's arms wrap around my neck, legs looping onto my hip, and we head to the kitchen. If Emma's much later we may need to reassess dinner all together. Maybe meet closer to her house, grab dinner along the way for all three of us.

"Snack?" Josephine's hands come away from my neck as I take a few steps, cupping my cheeks to gain my undivided attention. Blue eyes lock on my own, it's like looking in a mirror with the clearness in them.

"Dinner first, then a snack," compromising with an almost toddler is not for the faint of heart. If you don't stand your ground, she'll give you the puppy dog eyes, wobbly her bottom lip, and then you're on the receiving end of crocodile tears.

"No, no, no," Josephine stars winding up. I take a deep breath, ready to have a battle on my hand when my phone rings from on the barstool. I never thought I'd be happy for an interruption.

"Let's answer the phone, it might be your momma," that deters her away from a meltdown over food.

"Ma-ma!" Josephine claps her hands, I plop her on the counter, keeping one hand behind back just in case, grab my ringing phone, and see an unknown number on the screen.

"It's not momma, princess. Hold on just a second," I tell Josephine, her little grabby hands reaching for the device.

"Me want," yeah that's not going to happen. This could be a work call and while some people have no problem with a toddler. I can't say the same for others.

"Hello, this is Jameson," I answer the phone.

"Hello, am I speaking with Jameson Evans?" A male voice asks on the other end of the line.

"This is him," waiting to hear who the caller is.

"I'm deputy sergeant Smith calling from Lane County Highway Patrol regarding Emma Kline," I already know, there's no way not to. Still, I listen as he explains what happened. Emma died on impact, a semi lost control after a car cut him off. Emma tried to change lanes, but it was unavoidable when the blown tire from the semi barreled her way. It's an active investigation and asked if I would meet them at the hospital. It's only natural they would call me, I'm Emma's emergency contact. She's estranged from her sister, Leah. Even if they did call her, the likelihood of her answering is slim to none. That left me as the only option. I nod my head unsure if I'm actually responding when he says he'll meet me at the hospital. That's when it hits me, Josephine won't have Emma in her life anymore.

--

One Week Later

The past week has been a clusterfuck, Emma had a goddamn last will and testament. Josephine would go directly to me, no time sharing if Leah even remotely came back in the picture. Money set aside for school all through the years, her house would be sold, and the proceeds would go to me in order to help support our daughter. If she wasn't currently buried six feet in the dirt, I'd be giving her a ration of shit. Though to be fair Emma is an attorney, sorry was. I swallow the lump in my throat thinking about everything she's going to miss out on, Christ, it still feels like it's not real.

"How you doing big brother?" Matthew asks coming up beside me. We're at a hall where Emma's friends and work associates are currently mingling. My family is here too for that matter. It took a bit for my parents to understand that we were just friends, especially Mom. She thought we'd learn to love one another until she saw Emma and me around each other a few times. Then it clicked and she was happy both of us were okay doing the co-parenting gig. Leah should be here, at least to say her goodbyes, she isn't though. A reason I can't fathom, there's a lot of heartache where the Kline girls come from and it's a damn shame all the hard work Emma dealt with to get out from underneath her parents. Both of them were addicted to drugs and overdosed when she was a teenager, forcing her to grow up too damn early. Emma did her best with Leah, that didn't stop her sister from shitting all over it. The way Emma told the story, the second Leah hit eighteen, she dropped out of high school and hit the roads running. They talk every now and then but other than that, it's like they were two strangers.

"As good as can be expected, I guess," I rub a hand down my face, trying to clear the fog. Josephine's been asking for Emma, I've tried to explain to her that she's in the sky but try getting that through to a toddler, "What am I gonna do, man. I've got work piling up and I can't take the princess to work with me," my job as the owner of a land clearing company makes it kind of hard when I'm on a skid steer for a few hours a day. Sure, there are times she can come and work with me but on a few jobs, absolutely fucking not.

"You know, we'll take her and so will Mom and Dad. But I get it, she's going to have it tough without a female figure in her life. You ever think about hiring a nanny?" I look at my brother as if he's got two heads, a damn nanny, not freaking likely.

"I'll figure it out. Emma set up dates for schools to interview next week. That should help so she's not shipped around too much between us now," I pull at the tie, loosening its hold. The stress getting to me with everything that needs to get done. I'd have a drink or two, except I'm driving, and no damn way will I take a chance.

"Or you can take a look at Jojo now, she's over there with Shaun's sister, Kody," Matthew puts his hands in his pockets, and rocks back on his heels, acting like he isn't conniving a plan.

"The last thing I need right now is to confuse Josephine," my eyes move to the nearly two-year-old who has me wrapped around her finger. She's doing a puzzle with Kody, Shaun's younger sister, except she isn't so young anymore. Nope, she's all woman, dark hair, dark eyes, dark eyelashes, and a body that has me thinking of shit I have no right to.

"I'm just offering a suggestion. Kody is back, for good and is getting back on her feet. Not sure if she's looking for a permanent nanny position, it could work out for the both of you," my head tips to the side, really looking at Jo and Kody. My baby girl is laughing for the first time in a week, she's not asking question I've got no answers to, and she's not trying to get her dad to smile. Josephine is being her normal toddler self.

"Yeah, maybe," I grunt, meanwhile I'm eye fucking a woman that's gotta be ten years my senior, a friend of the family in some aspect yet tell that to my hard as fuck cock.

"Let me know if you need her number," Matthew claps my on the back and a smug smirk locked on his face. I'd say fuck you and knock the look off his mug if it weren't for the fact my eyes are glued to Kody.

Amazon

ABOUT THE AUTHOR

Tory Baker is a mom and dog mom, living on the coast of sunny Florida where she enjoys the sun, sand, and water anytime she can. Most of the time you can find her outside with her laptop, soaking up the rays while writing about Alpha men, sassy heroines, and always with a guaranteed happily ever after.

Sign up to receive her **Newsletter** for all the latest news!

Tory Baker's Readers is where you see and hear all of the news first!

ACKNOWLEDGMENTS

This is about to get very long and very wordy because that's just who I am. I've got so many people to thank and shout out that I hope no one is forgotten. When I set out about change this year, I was all freaking in. I'm extremely fortunate you all are taking this wild ride with me. The depth in these stories it fills my heart up with a joy I lost along the way and my cup couldn't runneth over without your support!

To my kids: A & A without you I'd be a shell of myself. You helped me find myself in a moment of darkness. Thank you for picking up the slack around the house while I was knee deep in this deadline, cooking, cleaning, and taking care of Remi (our big lug of a Weimaraner). I love you to infinity times infinity.

Jordan: Oh my lanta, the hand holding, the me calling you hysterically crying or laughing, day or night, good or bad. I love you bigger than outer space. If it weren't for you pushing me to write, to see the potential in me, I wouldn't be here.

Mayra: My sprinting partner extraordinaire. Girlfriend, we made it through 2022 ahead of schedule. One day I will fly my butt to California to hug you!

Julia: How do you deal with me and my extra sprinkling of commas? The real MVP, the one who deals with my scatterbrained self, missing deadlines, rescheduling like crazy, and the person I live vicariously through social media.

Amie Vermaas Jones: Thank you for always and I do mean always helping me on my last minute shit. It never fails that I'm sending you an SOS asking for your eyes. Beach days are happening and SOON!

Thank you for being here, reading, not just my books but any Author's stories. We do appreciate you more than you know, the reason why we can live out our dream is for readers, bloggers, bookstagrammers, bookmakers, Authors, and everyone in between. THANK YOU!

All this to say, I am and will always be forever grateful, love you all!

ALSO BY TORY BAKER

Men in Charge

Make Her Mine

Staking His Claim

Secret Obsession

Baring it All

Billionaire Playboys

Playing Dirty

Playing with Fire

Playing With Her

Playing His Games

Playing to Win

Vegas After Dark Series

All Night Long

Late Night Caller

One More Night

About Last Night

One Night Stand

Hart of Stone Family

Tease Me

Hold Me

Kiss Me

Please Me

Touch Me

Feel Me

Diamondback MC Second Gen.

Obsessive

Seductive

Addictive

Protective

Deceptive

Diamondback MC

Dirty

Wild

Bare

Wet

Filthy

Sinful

Wicked

Thick

Bad Boys of Texas

Harder

Bigger

Deeper

Hotter

Faster

Hot Shot Series

Fox

Cruz

Jax

Saint

Getting Dirty Series

Serviced (Book 1)

Primed (Book 2)

Licked (Book 3)

Hammered (Book 4)

Nighthawk Security

Never Letting Go (Easton and Cam's story)

Claiming Her (Book 1)

Craving More (Book 2)

Sticky Situations (Travis and Raelynn's story)

Needing Him (Book 3)

Only His (Book 4)

Carter Brothers Series

Just One Kiss

Just One Touch

Just One Promise

Finding Love Series

A Love Like Ours

A Love To Cherish

A Love That Lasts

Stand Alone Titles

Nailed

Going All In

What He Wants

Accidental Daddy

Love Me Forever

Gettin' Lucky

It's Her Love

Meant To Be

Breaking His Rules

Can't Walk Away

Carried Away

In Love With My Best Friend

Must Be Love

Sweet As Candy

Falling For Her

All Yours

Sweet Nothings Book 3—Tory Baker

Loving The Mountain Man

Crazy For You

Trick— The Kelly Brothers

Friend Zoned

His Snow Angel

223 True Love Ln.

Hard Ride

Slow Grind

1102 Sugar Rd.

The Christmas Virgin

Taking Control

Unwrapping His Present

Tempting the Judge

Made in United States
Orlando, FL
15 July 2025

62997240R00187